Killer Word

A Novel by Dorothy Sample

Produced in the United States of America

First edition

Released in 2019

Sample Graphics

12901 Main Street

Garden Grove, CA 92840

Killer Word

A *Words With Friends Thriller*

by Dorothy Sample

Chapter 1

THE CELLPHONE

You know that annoying sound. That buzzing sound. We all know it. You stick your phone on vibrate and throw it in your purse, your pocket, on the counter or next to the bed. You're driving and you try to ignore the buzzing or the ringing, but you have that nagging feeling, "Who wants me? Is it important? What if somebody died?" Okay, that's probably not likely.

While you're trying to throw dinner together, it buzzes gently on the counter, bouncing and pushing itself to the edge, threatening to drop to the tiled floor. In the morning when it rings from its home on the nightstand at a quarter to seven, calling to you to pick up, the thought occurs to you – is it really six forty-five? Damned if you do and damned if you don't because now that you have it, everyone expects instant communication. They now expect your voice or a detailed text outlining your agenda for the day - or, even worse, *their* agenda.

It all started with a nifty little flip top version. I was happy as a clam - excuse the pun. It was simple, easy to use and oh, yes, ridiculed by my tech-savvy friends.

"Hey, just text me," they would say.

"Nope, I don't text".

"Let me see that. Wow, this thing doesn't even have a keyboard!"

And then I received a flyer in the mail advertising a phone that was much better and more modern than mine. I gave in to the peer pressure and the hype and became the proud owner of a phone much smarter than me.

So now, it's the constant humming, buzzing, ringing, texting and photo sharing. Oh yes, now I "Instagram" - lowering myself to the level of snapping pictures of the food I'm about to eat - sending it on to other foodie friends.

"Really? Looks delish."

"Love that restaurant - who are you there with?"

If you should happen to turn the device off, or if the battery goes dead, you never hear the end of it.

"Why didn't you reply to my text? I was worried about you. Why do you have a cell phone if you're never going to answer it?"

Like it or not, sooner or later, it becomes your best friend and goes with you everywhere. A constant juggling act now begins.

This brings me to problem number two. My device looks like it has been through the war. It is shattered on one corner and has a crack running through its face. But I've bonded with the little guy, he's been so abused that I couldn't possibly replace him.

I've begun making excuses for him, telling others that I've recently dropped him. This lie has now gone on for months.

In the beginning, a friend suggested I needed one of those little covers to protect it and gave me a leopard print case that looked like a fashion statement. Would it go with

3

everything? Would it clash or look too fancy? It turned out to be perfectly practical until the print started rubbing off, so I ditched it for a hot pink polka dot number, but it didn't fit well and kept turning the phone off. When I finally got rid of the cover idea, the dropping and bouncing on hard surfaces went into full swing.

My friend Susan and I do lunch on Mondays, usually preceded by a quick early text. However, it's never quick with Sue –

"Where should we go?"

"How do we get there?"

"Did you say twelve or twelve thirty?"

"Can I bring my niece Chloe?"

"Do you think they have grilled cheese?"

By the time the texting is over, I'm not sure if we'll have anything left to say. On this particular Monday, we finally made it there, after two or three more texts.

"I'm running late."

"Get a table, but not inside - it's beautiful out and Chloe

will not be so restless outside."

I've thrown on something casual for the event: jeans, t-shirt, a cardigan, flats and my great big electric blue bag for a pop of color.   I don't have much fashion sense, but after all, it's lunch outside with an eight-year-old.

About that cell phone – since he's my best friend, I've given him a name. I've named him Bob, just Bob. Actually, he's not my best friend, or should I say my BFF. My BFF is Brad.

 We've been together two years and he get's me. Who could be so lucky? Susan, no doubt, wants to grill me on the Brad thing today. "When? When? When? Put a ring on it," and all that. Or she'll suggest we take it to the next level - move in together, 'consolidate' as she puts it. Same questions, different Monday. To change the subject, I will snap pictures of my beautiful food and text them to Kelly, my foodie friend…it just kills Susan when I do that.

Chapter 2

BRAD

About Brad, in case you are wondering about him. I literally bumped into him one day, because I'm a little clumsy. It was one of those cell phone-in-hand moments. I should say, phone, keys, purse, hot coffee in hand moments. It was the whole sit-com scenario - boy meets girl, girl spills coffee, she's embarrassed, but he doesn't seem to mind. The gallant prince buys her new coffee, just the way she likes it, then sets the princess down, calming her and making her feel secure. What a guy. About twenty minutes later, we knew the basics about each other and he put my number on his cell and the rest is history. This might all sound a little boring, but sometimes boring can be good, skipping the drama and games. My friends actually thought it was romantic and crazy. Susan was her usual skeptical self, but she soon met him and agreed Brad was a keeper. This is also why she thinks we need to take it to the next level. The guy has a steady job, an even temper, he's handsome, solid – so why waste time? He works at a computer all day, which I thought was a little boring at first. I soon realized that what I lack in computer skills, Brad more than makes up for.

Brad lives just a few miles away and so we quickly fell into a casual routine of meeting at the corner pub or café, or preparing our own meals and eating in. Most evenings, we watch an old movie or the news, and then around ten, he pushes himself out the door or I push him, with a quick peck on the cheek…safe, very safe.

Brad likes all his ducks in a row; he's just that kind of a guy. He's the boyfriend every parent would love, which is kind of ironic because I don't have a parent to care about who I'm with. It's nice to think that if they were here, they'd love him.

Brad doesn't talk much about his work, but he loves to kick around ideas. Brad wishes he could start his own business, but his employer knows they have a good thing going and they treat him very well because of it. It's hard to walk away from a regular pay check.

He's not the kind of guy to clear the table or help do the dishes, but he always offers. You can tell he'd rather not and that's o.k. too, because guys don't always do it right anyway. We both have long work schedules and his thing is hitting the couch to finish up his day. I can't see my life these days without him….he's definitely the one. He knows I don't care about the bling and would never want a big over-done wedding, and he feels the same. Brad's definitely not the tux type. Maybe I could get him into a new suit, but that would be the maximum. Susan would just die.

We would both like to travel and start our life together going somewhere we've never been. We talk about travel a lot, but mostly we talk about starting a business that we could do together. I lost the best job I ever had a year or so before I met Brad. Out of complete desperation and slightly behind in everything, I racked my brain for what I could do to make a living that wouldn't cost much to start up. So, after discussing this at length with my hairdresser, Pam, she told me there was a lady that she knew who might help solve my problem. Her husband had recently died and she needed help with errands and chores, being no longer able to drive,. And so, Rita became the start of a personal assistance service that I do for several ladies. Another lady named Martha was soon added to my client list who also needed help. It was a start for me and made me self-sufficient once again. Brad admired the fact that I jumped right into doing something I enjoyed when the search for a job had become bleak.

Now I mentioned Brad is good looking – there's a broad spectrum of good looking - so I'll explain. He has that clean shaven boyish look that's hard to resist. He doesn't know what GQ is, nor would he care. His idea of shopping is, pull it off the rack - this one's fine. No trying it on, it's such a waste of time. Now, I'm not exactly a fashion plate myself, so why should I care? He's tall, about six foot, thin but not too thin, and has lots of sun streaked blond hair.

Some guys meet down at the gym and shoot a few baskets and talk about the game on Sunday, Brad's not really into that. If he's forced into the big super bowl game party, he just picks a team and fakes it. He'll have a lot of fun doing it too, because you'll think it's his all-time favorite team.

When I'm stressed out, Brad can usually make me laugh. He has a great sense of humor and I think it is his best attribute. We both agree we need to laugh our way through a lot of the stuff that just happens in life.

A couple of weeks ago, Brad appeared at my apartment driving a brand-new car. It must have been one of his proudest moments ever. He didn't want a huge payment, so he planned this purchase, over time, working and saving. This is the way he does things, almost old fashioned. I just have to laugh when I see him with that car, he is so in love with it. It was really important to him that I love it too – and I do.

Brad has a great Mom and Dad. I met them when they came to visit and loved them right away. It was evident that they have a great relationship and have been a real influence on his life. He has one older brother who is a real pill, but then again, so do I. We have that in common.

Chapter 3

ME

So, I haven't told you much about me. My name is Diane, but it usually works into Di. I never really appreciated my nickname until Lady Di came along and then it became so royal. I thought it sounded too much like "DIE" or should I say just like "DIE". Death is such an unpleasant subject to be connected to my name. Someone asks my name and I reply, "Di." See what I mean? It is short and to the point - like me. Diane is such a common name that all through High School, I became 'Doo-Dah' to my friends, so ending up Di is not so bad. Brad shortens it all the way to "D", that's o.k. too because it all sounds good coming from him.

My upbringing was similar to Brad's, except mine was to the extreme. I grew up with Ozzie and Harriet. Mom wore an apron while vacuuming the house and Dad came home with a briefcase, dressed in a suit and tie. They were great though, never raising their voices to discuss anything. Oh, I take that back, they had one fight. I cried all night because I thought it meant that a divorce would follow. I was about nine and that was exactly what happened to my friend Becky from school. Her parents fought and then they got a divorce. To this day I have no idea what my parent's fight was about, but they never had another one – at least not in my presence.

I have one brother two years older than me. As kids we did all the usual stuff. Mostly we did boy stuff because boys don't do girl stuff. We'd spend summer afternoons burning up bugs with a magnifying glass or clipping playing cards with clothes pins to our bicycle spokes to make noise. I have a lot of good memories about those days.

Mom died of cancer shortly after I graduated from college. Dad died a year later of a broken heart. That might sound strange, but Dad was a little older than most of my friend's parents. Growing up I was always aware of that fact but had no idea how that would affect my life later. They were the glue of the family holding my brother and I together. With them gone my brother and I just drifted apart. Now we rarely see each other and don't stay in touch. I lost them way too soon. I always carry a piece of them with me. Always.

Chapter 4

CALIFORNIA GIRL

I don't have to dress up for my job, as a matter of fact being my own boss, I set my own standard. My uniform is comfortable jeans, shirts, flats. I think you could call it California casual. The weather is so nice, a light sweater is about all is needed year-round. My shoulder length hair is easy either pulled back or hanging loose, depending on the mood.

I live in a place where I guess some people would love to live. I've been here all my life and maybe I take it for granted. I have palm trees and sand in my backyard and on a quiet night can hear the ocean. I grew up here and probably will never leave. It's called Huntington Beach and is nicknamed Surf City, for obvious reasons. So, we get lots of tourists and surfers from all over, making an interesting mix. It's overpriced, with too much traffic and pedestrians swarming all over, but I call it home. Good weather makes it a real transient area; summer people, winter people and a small percentage of year-round residents like me. It's quite possible to get hooked on nearly perfect year-round weather and just stay. The little town has lots of small shops, cafes and bars. It has a small-town feel, locals know locals and pretend to be annoyed by the tourists but in most cases, they are the livelihood of the town.

I live in what I call my little apartment, but it is actually a tri-plex with three small one-bedroom units, facing three identical units with a walkway right up the middle. This is the smallest place I've ever lived in. I think of it as fewer places to misplace Bob. It was built in the forties and with the price of California beach property, such small, cozy units will never be built again. Despite the age of the structure, the owners keep it up and it could be described as cute. I live in unit number two; right between a 'stick in the mud' in number three, who wouldn't know me if I ran smack into him and number one, occupied by Kaye. Kaye is an older woman who serves as my free security system.

Kaye knows every move I make, when I come and when I go. She usually verifies that fact by peaking her head out as I pass by on the walkway. Kaye's cool though; she never interferes but I'm always aware that she's got one eye on me. Oh, and she has one eye on Brad and his comings and goings also. No one gets past Kaye. Another reason for separate abodes. Kaye would be so disappointed in me.

If I spend any extra money I usually spend it on my little apartment. I have a frustrated decorator gene surging thru my blood. I can't pass up some used item to paint and give a new life. Sometimes these things are perfect for the apartment and sometimes I just pass them on to someone who admires it and needs it more than I do. I don't want to look like a hoarder - I could verge on that.

Brad moved here from the east coast. His company offered him a transfer and he admits that he was just ready for a change. The offer came along at the sad finish of a relationship. I don't ask a lot of questions about it...do I really want to know? He needed a new start, end of story. As it turned out there were more perks to the move than he thought.   He doesn't have to shovel snow anymore, he loves the sunshine, his new workmates and, oh yes - me.

Before I met Brad I had a lot of short stints of, what you might call love, with guys that could probably be classified as jerks. For what seemed like forever I just kept finding them. if they were strange, I found them and brought them home like little stray puppies. Brad was a welcome sight that day with coffee all down the front of his crisp, freshly starched shirt. Oops. Unlike the previously mentioned list of guys, he actually called - the day after, I might add. Then to my surprise he kept calling. I felt bad about our first encounter and bought him a new shirt - you know what coffee can do.

I'm sure moving all that distance he must have been lonely at times, but I never sensed it at all. Brad has the ability to fit in anywhere. My friends have become his. His happy nature and outgoing personality allows him to fit in with every circumstance.   In no time at all he became this California girl's California guy - he is a real local.

Chapter 5

SUSAN, CHLOE AND LUNCH

As I expected the grill started early on. Susan jumped right in.

"When? When? When? What were we waiting for?"

She even turned it around, saying if he didn't marry me I should dump him and move on. This was the point for Bob to come to the rescue. Remember Bob? I took him out and began taking photos of a Punky Brewster-like child with a hunk of grilled cheese hanging out of her mouth. Then I moved on to pictures of half eaten food and anything else that seemed worthy - and some things not.

At some point in my photo shoot, Susan noticed Bob. I think she noticed the poor guy several other times but she had refrained from saying anything until now.

"Di, that thing looks horrible, isn't it time you get a new

phone? It's disgusting, your attachment to it is ridiculous you really need to move on."

 So, I'm just stuck with Brad and Bob, what could be worse? Now don't get me wrong, I really love this girl but when she feels the need to redirect your life you might as well sit back and listen until the rant is over. On the brighter side, she grabbed Bob away from me to point out some function on him I didn't know about yet. Most of the time I could use some help in these areas, so that was good.

 "Hey Di, why don't you play *Words With Friends*? You're going to need something to do after you dump Brad."

She proceeded to set me up right there at Sweet's Café, so I could play this game.

Monday the twenty-third of February I was given my very own user name, *Diwordmaster*. My life would never be the same. It almost sounded German or like I knew what I was doing. Susan is so clever to come up with that on the spur of the moment, since my last name is Masters. This users name is not what I would pick for myself, but I'd never figure out how to change it. I guess she thought she was helping me out because of being a fidgety person. I've always got to be doing something. Usually while watching TV I'm doing something else. I was never good at crossword and find-a-word seemed a bit boring, so I often would grab a Sudoko puzzle book. This drove Susan nuts to see me with one of those books; she'd just rip it right out of my hand. What can I say she's my BFF you've got to love the girl. Brad on the other hand, who I always feel verges on genius, can't walk and chew gum simultaneously, let alone watch T.V. and do a puzzle, but it never seems to bother him that I can.

We finished lunch after a complete *Words With Friends* lesson. I tried to act like I wasn't interested but my competitive spirit had been sparked. Susan, whose username is *SASSYSUE*, was my first opponent. I might like it, I thought to myself, I'll check it out later.

Susan means well, she would do anything for me. She has such a sense of pride when she has her say. It was easy to see that it really made her day to give me so much needed direction. What a pal.

Chloe was busy looking at the parade of people on the boardwalk while eating her grilled cheese and fries. She was somewhat quiet and seemed like a pleasant little girl. I'd smile at her every once and a while and she would return the smile. Apparently, she was observing more than the sights because when we gave our goodbye hugs she had something to say. I leaned down and in a hushed tone she asked,

"Di, where are you going to dump Brad at?"

Kids take things so literal. I tried not to laugh.

"See you next week if not sooner."

"Yes, and don't forget what I told you."

"Huh? Oh yes, it is time for me to move on."

Chapter 6

EVENINGS WITH THE WORDMASTER

Now Bob has a new annoying noise that I need to pay attention to. He makes a little ring to let me know that a "friend" has played a word and wants me to join in and play a word in return. Somehow, friends have other friends and soon the game is in full swing. At nearly any time of the day someone is playing this game. They come from all over.

As a kid, my family traveled to Texas every summer to visit my Aunt and Uncle. It seemed everyone in the family played Scrabble. On those long summer days visiting relatives, it was much too hot to play outside, so the card table was set up twenty-four seven and we had either a Scrabble or a Domino game going. I was good at neither.

Words With Friends however, is much better, because your opponent can't see what you are doing and you can change things around with impunity. Besides that, I'd like to think I have a better vocabulary than I did when I was twelve. Now I can make up words and not get dinged for doing it. I DO make up words - like if drain is a word why isn't *redrain* a word?

I soon learned that several of my real friends also played, but who you could count on to play regularly was pretty hit and miss. It was usually a word here and a word there, unless schedules matched or someone happened to be bored at the same time as you. With my job I often have wait times and it's a perfect time to whip out Bob, looking very official, and play a word or two. A word in the morning with coffee catches me up with the insomniacs. Like I mentioned before, there is that evening unwind time that I need to do something. The spooky thing is when I hear that little sound indicating there is a player waiting for me at three in the morning as Bob sits on his charger. I'm not addicted, not at all, but somebody out there is.

We're in March now and it's a funny month in California. It's a month that California can't decide what to do with; should we have a late winter or an early summer this year.

Here by the beach we get a lot of early morning fog that breaks late morning or sometimes not until noon. We get warm afternoons and sometimes even a surprise shower. It was a Tuesday evening and we were all cozy in the apartment with popcorn, Brad with his laptop and me with my "friends". It just happened to be one of those crazy unexpected weather fronts; it was pouring outside. On this particular rainy evening, no one wanted to play. Could it be that they all ran out and got a life all at once?

I gathered some regular players that I suppose are just like me, multi-tasking in front of the T.V. Others might be moms that have just tucked the kids in. Some come in and out a word at a time some play a game straight thru. A friend in Utah named Martha plays on a fairly regular basis. She's called *MISTINK*, I had a hard time figuring that one out, until she told me it had to do with Peter Pan. Martha told me once that it was never too late to have a happy childhood, so that all fits. Another friend named Kathy goes by *KATDANCIN*, I assume she likes to dance? One of my very savvy friends, Alysia, goes by *ALYSIAROCKS*. By the way she does, I haven't been able

27

to beat her yet. But mostly I'm playing people I don't even know. I can only imagine what kind of a person 36DONUTS is, but I like donuts, so I would probably like her, or him - she could be a him, who knows? But on this night they were all gone. I switched over to instagram to catch up on what people were doing. I found a few foodie pictures from *COOKINKELLY* and followed another friend who is traveling all over to places I'll probably never see. Brad seemed very engrossed in whatever he was doing on his laptop. Sometimes he had to catch up on work he brought home to finish in the evenings. So, I was back to "Words." Where are you guys?

There's a little feature to "nudge" people so they get the annoying ring tone of their choice and reminds them that someone wants to play. I nudged and still no one responded. Then I noticed the "start a game" feature. It said THEY would find me a player – how nice. I wait for a new player. Now, not that there's not already way too much texting going on in the world, there's one more feature that allows you to "chat" with your opponent. I personally don't have the time or desire to talk as well as play and most of the players seem to feel the same way, or at least respect that view. Now and then I'll get a chat but it's usually after someone makes some phenomenal 96-point word, the kind of word you don't even know exists. The chat after such a play is more like a pat on the back, good job, unbelievable word, or great game! Then I heard the noise I was waiting for, I have a new friend, lucky me. His or her name is *KILLERWORD*. Sometimes I play a real 'killer' word myself, cute name. *KILLERWORD* played first. I played second after a pretty good first word. It wasn't spectacular but good enough to keep up. Sometimes, between words I like to do little chores, but tonight the words are flying. This guy, assuming he's a guy, is pretty good at this, the problem is he really *knows* he's good. He wants to do a lot of chatting, or should I say he wants to do a lot of bragging. Every good word, and he had many of them, was followed with how good he is at this game, and how I couldn't beat him. This was weird and a bit intimidating. In the end, he won, but not by much, which surprised me, because nearly every word he played was a word I'd never heard of. It was as if he made these words up and then they really were words! If you do this long enough you discover new things about the English language. Did you know aa is considered a word? I tried that with every other letter in the alphabet – it doesn't work with any other letter. Killer wants to chat, something contrite like "nice try". Hmm, whatever does that mean? The chat struck me wrong; It had a taunting sound to it. Totally out of character I responded.

" Yes, but I'd rather win."

Suddenly a war had started.

"That's going to be pretty impossible since I win 99 percent of my games," he responded.

What was this guy saying? No one is that good. Oddly many of his chat words were misspelled.

"What an arrogant Bozo." I muttered.

Brad looked my way but I barely noticed. My competitive juices were flowing and I wasn't about to just quit. This guy wasn't a casual game player, he was taking this very seriously. Words were flying, if there was a lull the chat would start.

"You can't lose if you don't play," he taunted.

Those were fighting words, forget quick breaks, it was word – on, we play – nonstop all evening! He took a little time to explain that he had a break in his job because of a freak snow storm. I responded by bragging myself that I don't have to worry about snow slowing me down, I have perfect weather in Huntington Beach California. I was getting too competitive by saying that, but he made me do it.

I tried several different strategies: play close to the middle - don't give him any chance to get close to any triples - don't set him up for any plays. Nothing was working very well until we finally tied a game. I leapt out of my seat with a victory arm pump only to find out they gave HIM the game! Funny thing about this game and I still don't understand it, but some weird rule gave the win to him. I looked it up and there were plenty of people upset about this rule. Killer was pretty smug about it. Killer already knew this rule – Killer had been playing way too long. So, without missing a beat, we're right into the next game. I played my best, but it was probably dumb luck that I finally managed to win. Killer did not take my win graciously. In fact, this guy was a real bad looser. He began to give excuses for why he lost. I guess I was messing up his stats. There goes his 99 percent winning streak. Who on earth keeps track of their *Words With Friends* stats? Killer does.

I assumed at this point, Killer went to bed. It was only 10 pm. He was either really old, or living in another time zone. 10 pm would be 1 am back East, so I chose that. It felt good to me that there might be some distance between us. At the close of the evening we were four to one, with that tie thing still up in the air as far as I was concerned. Brad clicked his laptop closed, and looked my way.

"Wow you were quiet tonight, good game?"

"Well sort of, I'm playing some guy who really thinks he's hot stuff."

We both laughed and stretched after being curled up all evening. Personally, I barely moved out of my spot at all. Brad headed for the door,

"I've got an early morning appointment - see you

tomorrow night, O.K.? How about we get some of that good Chinese after work over at Wong's?"

Wong's sounded good to me, we like that place. We are both pretty easy to please; we agree on most all of the small stuff - big stuff too.

I must admit, that night I wondered if I had crossed the line by stringing along three guys; Brad, Bob and Killer. I had to laugh at myself, and at that thought, as I crawled into my bed. All these guys and me alone with cold sheets.

Chapter 7

HOW TO CHEAT

Brad came by after work and we took "the car" to
Wong's. We could have walked but Brad was in new
love with the car. I was in my usual casual attire and I
wondered for a moment if the car might require me to
dress up a little. I thought better of it and decided "she"
would just have to get over it. Walking out we got stopped
by Kaye, she had noticed the car and was cooing over how
pretty she looked. Brad in a teasing manner said he'd take
her out for a spin later and Kaye just waved him on and
went back in. I started feeling like a kid going to the prom
expecting someone to jump out of the bushes and start
shooting pictures paparazzi style.

We arrived at Wong's about ten minutes later, after several
trips around the block looking for parking, which seemed
to please Brad, rather than being an irritation. The owner

met us at the door with a polite bow at the waist as he always did.

"Good evening Mr. Brad and Miss Diane."

We always responded by greeting him as Mr. Wong, although I'm not sure that is his real name. He seated us at our usual booth and we ordered our usual favorite dishes. It was just that kind of homey place, very comfortable. Settling in, I heard that noise from Bob in my purse. I tried to ignore it, because it was so early I was pretty sure it was Killer, he wasn't done with me yet. I was keenly aware of this time difference, he wanted to get started earlier and finish early too. Again, I was thinking that he lived far away and that was fine with me. After all we don't need any more killers on the west coast – ever listen to the news?

Brad was talking about some work he needed to do tonight when we get back to the apartment and added that it sounded like I did too, pointing at my purse sitting on the booth seat and laughing.

"Yeah, I have to go home and kill the Killer. You know I

have the weirdest feeling this guy cheats, but for the life of me I don't know how. You can stop and look up a word but that takes time and he plays lightning fast. If there is a lull in playing at all, he chats about how good he is. Oh, he is good, his words are genius. In every game he is able to play one or more words that take all seven tiles. Most of his words are words that I'm sure you've never heard of, I haven't."

About that time I pulled Bob out and sure enough, there he was. Brad looked thoughtful,

"Oh, I'm sure there is a way to cheat. We'll have to look and see."

"But what's the fun in that?"

While I'm looking at the game I notice Killer has a chat for me. His chat is an explanation for his loss of a game. It seems when he is driving his big rig it's hard to concentrate on the game. What? This guy has to be kidding! Who in their right mind could drive a big rig and play *Words With Friends* all at the same time? Since I do have a conscience I responded.

"Sounds dangerous, I don't want to be responsible for an accident on the highway, please don't play me while you drive."

The conversation confirmed he is a guy who lives in Atlanta Georgia. Interesting, but more than I needed to know. It was starting to make me feel nervous and his comments felt a little invasive.

We returned home and both of us flopped on the sofa, foot to foot each of us getting our special end and favorite throw pillow. Forget about getting hungry in an hour, I am stuffed and I know it is game time with no breaks. So out come our devices, Brad with his laptop and me and Bob, fully charged. Sure enough, Killer had impatiently already sent messages urging me to get started so I could lose. This guy is like a shark in bloody water. I passed and made him make the first play - my big strategy. I'm not sure that going second actually helped, but I felt it gave me more options. He proceeded to use all seven tiles for his first word. Seventy-two points, I could be in trouble.

"Unbelievable!" I uttered out loud, not really meaning to. Across the sofa came a response.

38

"He's Cheating."

Brad slowly got up and moved down to my end of the sofa so I could see his laptop. There it was. He had discovered an entire website designed for players to cheat their way through *Words With Friends* and be a winner. On the main gameboard, you type in the plays and your tiles and *bingo,* it gives you all your choices, as well as how many points you will make.

"Now really, what is the fun in that?" I exclaimed.

"If he's not using this website, I've found several others just like it," Brad said.

Brad just shrugged his shoulders with that cute grin as he got up to go back to his spot.

I thought it was interesting, but I quickly dismissed the idea. You see, I'm just honest to a fault, like who would catch me? What would they do to me if they did? Besides for some reason I'm still thinking I can beat this Bozo. I continued to lose all evening. When Brad left that evening he could see I was frustrated with my relaxing diversion.

"Hey, I've got an idea. This weekend let's play this guy

together and cheat our way to victory."

I never thought of Brad as a cheater and he looked a little too excited about the prospect, but it would be fun. Right there in the living room we high- fived our plan - It's a cheating date.

Chapter 8

CHEATERS PROSPER

Saturday morning started foggy and dreary as it does sometimes. It seemed like a great morning to be hanging out at home. I put on some coffee and jumped in the shower, expecting Brad around ten. We were in no hurry we had all day with nothing to do but cheat. This should be fun, first I would make us a big breakfast and then we would kill Killer.

Around ten, Brad came in to the smell of coffee, hash browns, eggs and toast. Brad loved a good breakfast, and this was one like he would commonly order if we went out. Brad's broad smile of approval was evidence that he was very pleased.

With no time wasted he ceremoniously popped out the laptop and fired it up with a mouthful of breakfast in his mouth. I think he went home last night and did a little homework. He was ready to win.

I was a bit apprehensive. What if cheating made me look too good and I would look like I was cheating? Killer might notice that I got a lot better overnight. I also didn't want to stoop to this guy's level. Another part of me wanted to bring him down. Cheating just once would be okay, I reasoned, because he was SO egotistical.

I grabbed Bob off his charger and went right to the game. There he was, waiting. I passed and let him go first. Brad typed *KILLER'S* word in on his game board, then he typed my letters in. My options appeared on the screen. I was given four words I could use, as well as how many points each word was worth. This was certainly a different way to scrabble. *KILLER* and I were racking up points and I couldn't help but think that we were both at the very same "cheaters" website. It was just one cheater playing another cheater and the winner would be the person who happened to get the best tiles.

Early in the afternoon *KILLER* chatted that he had to go to work, adding that he wouldn't be back on Sunday until after Church.

"Oh, this is just great," I exclaimed, "My new friend is a church-going, cheating, truck driver; what could be weirder?"

Brad closed his laptop.

"Let's take a walk, I'm getting a bit tired of this guy anyway, we'll get him tomorrow."

I couldn't believe that Brad was into this enough to finish him off 'after church.' We had a good day of cheating with a lot of laughs about the words we came up with and we didn't feel guilty about it at all.

By now it was beautiful outside and we headed down to the beach. We needed a nice stretch and the walk was perfect. We ended up at one of our favorite pubs for some chips and salsa and a couple beers. The two of us had such fun together and although we had friends we could call to join us we were just fine - the two of us.

Sunday came and went and yes, I won. We played as soon as KILLER returned from church. I refrained about asking him about the sermon, but I really did think about it. I kept thinking how funny it would be if it was about honesty.

43

He chatted frequently, bragging when he won and making excuses when he didn't. He had nasty remarks about my lucky wins and always shifted attention away from any plays that we made that were truly amazing. I achieved my goal and decided that I didn't need this anymore, after all, this was supposed to be just for fun, a relaxing diversion, not tense and irritating.

Now, there is still a group of us playing and the leader board shows all our positions as far as wins. I check the board from time to time; the game scores run from Sunday to Sunday. Killer is always there on the board, usually in the top three. I wondered if he was cheating all my friends. I felt like I created a monster because I was the one who invited him to play and now, I didn't know how to get rid of him. He actually challenged me one or two more times, but I ignored him. I was done; I did not need the irritation.

Chapter 9

THE GIFT

Sometime in June, I came dragging into my apartment with groceries and noticed Kaye walking up the walk after me. Out of breath, she explained that the postman had left me a package and I wasn't home to receive it. It was just a tiny package and he didn't want it to get lost, so Kaye said she'd make sure I got it. Kaye stood for a minute, looking at me, waiting for me to rip it open. I'm pretty sure she was dying to know what was inside. I noticed it was shipped from Amazon. My mind drifted briefly to Brad, he was the only one I could think of who would get me a gift. Then I thought logically, he would never send me something in the mail, I see him almost every day. He has given me gifts before and would always ship them to himself, check them out and then deliver them in person. Part of the reason for that was so he could see my expression.

I was saved by Bob because he started ringing at the perfect time, almost on cue. I grabbed Bob from the counter and thanked Kaye profusely at the same time, hoping she wouldn't stand there through my conversation, so she could find out the details of the box and who sent it. The phone call turned out to be urgent. Rita, one of the ladies that I work for, had fallen and was being transported to the hospital. She needed me there. I was listed on her medical records as the one to call, living much closer to her than any of her family members. At this point, I was literally throwing groceries in the refrigerator and freezer. Anything that didn't need to be kept cold would have to sit out until later. I am exactly twelve minutes from our local hospital and I know all the short cuts. Kaye stayed long enough to get the drift that I was needed. I vaguely remember her fading away around the corner of the doorway, while I continued my conversation and took a few quick notes. I finished with the groceries, grabbed a sweater, purse, Bob and flew out the door.

In my rush, I did not bring the package and much later while I was in the middle of the hospital waiting game, I wished that I had. My evening became very long, flipping through a few old magazines and walking around over waxed halls in shoes I didn't mean to wear for such an extended period of time.

I called Brad around five to let him know what was going on and to tell him we'd have to cancel our plans because I wasn't going to be home any time soon. Then I proceeded to find a vending machine and got some Fritos and a candy bar for dinner.

I spent some time thinking about the box. I made a mental list of who might send me something. I arrived at the same answer with Susan as with Brad. I see her every Monday, why mail me a box? It would make sense that it would be someone that didn't live close, possibly my friend in Utah who I play words with. There really was no sense in over-thinking it, there was probably a simple explanation.

Much later in the evening I got the good news. After many tests and x-rays, the doctor came to let me know my lady, Rita, would be fine. They gave her some pain medication and got her comfortable. She had no broken bones but would be pretty sore tomorrow. They decided to keep her for the night and I could pick her up tomorrow after they checked her in the morning.

As I went into her room I could see she was out for the count. It was late. I would call her daughter in the morning, then come back over and take it from there.

Within a few minutes, I was out to the parking structure in my car and on my way home. As I turned the key, it hit me - I was exhausted. My day had been very long. I pulled up in front of my apartment, it was dark and quiet. I pulled off my flats and tiptoed down the walkway to my door. I didn't want to wake Kaye, she would have heart failure over the time; it was 1 a.m.

I hadn't planned on being gone so long. I was hungry, but I didn't care. Sleep was the only thing on my mind. I didn't think about the groceries still sitting out, or about my little package. I went straight to bed and instantly to sleep. When I woke up, I think I was lying exactly in the same position I landed the night before.

I started to move around the apartment, I was running late. Brad would be here soon and I still had things on the kitchen counter to put away. I opted to start with a shower. Brad and I could visit while I put food away - he'd probably even give me a hand.

Sure enough, about the time I walked into the living room, Brad was letting himself in. I was relieved that he walked in with two cups of coffee and a small bag of muffins. I started to put things away as I was catching him up with last night's events and for the first time since yesterday afternoon, my eyes landed on the small box. For reasons I can't even explain, I opened the silverware drawer and just pushed the box in and closed the drawer. After thinking on it last night, I was pretty sure the box wasn't from Brad and I wanted to know what it was before I told him about it. If Brad were the gift giver, he would never be able to keep quiet about it this long.

Bob started ringing and I had to take the call; it was the hospital wanting me to pick up Rita. We both left at the same time and I didn't have the opportunity to go back and get the box. By now, my curiosity was driving me crazy, but I'd probably have to wait until tonight.

I got Rita settled in her home, making sure she had

everything she needed for the evening. I made a trip to the pharmacy and to the store for groceries that would be easy to prepare. When I got back, I straightened up and picked up the mail. Everything was in order, so I called her daughter and assured her everything was O.K. By early afternoon, Rita was exhausted and sent me on my way, so she could get some rest.

For a change, I was done with my day earlier than usual and had a few errands of my own to run. My mind kept drifting to the box and I found myself rushing through everything, so I could go home and discover its contents. I'm usually a patient person, but I found myself finger drumming through red lights. I rewrote my mental "to do" list in my head, removing anything that I could do tomorrow. Finally, I pulled up to my apartment, finding no place to park as usual, I ended up down the block. Now, if I could rush past Kaye's door without being stopped, I could solve my little mystery. I've learned that very few things go as we plan. Out of unit number one pops a gray-headed lady named Kaye and today, she wants to talk. Probably a more accurate statement would be "she wants to ask questions." My schedule over the last few days has been a bit questionable, so I guess she's just doing her job. I did the best I could to satisfy her and not spend the entire afternoon doing it. About the time I was shifting my weight impatiently, Bob began screaming in my purse; good ol' Bob has saved me again. I hurriedly excused myself, telling her the call might be my sick customer Rita, knowing full well she wouldn't be calling. I edged to my door, giving Kaye a wave and I could hear her heave a sigh.

The call that saved me was coming from Susan and she too needed to talk and ask questions. Strangely enough, after a few minutes, our connection started "breaking up"- can you believe it? That is what I call one of the great joys of having a friend like Bob.

Finally, back in my living room and by myself (not counting Bob), I rushed across the room to the kitchen drawer. I ripped through the outside box to a slightly smaller ring sized box. Suddenly, I was frightened; what if this was a ring and Brad mistakenly sent it to me instead of himself. This was silly and ridiculous thinking, he's a smart guy; Brad would never do that. When and if the day ever came, I think we would be practical and shop together for a nice simple wedding band; he would want me to have exactly what I wanted. I took a breath and opened the box. A small piece of cotton was covering a chain with a wooden trinket on it; it looked like a scrabble game tile with the letter "D" on it. Cute, I thought to myself, a little bit corny, but cute. That was it, no note, nothing, just the necklace. I didn't mean to be ungrateful, but I guess I had built this up in my mind and I felt a little let down. The big question wasn't answered by opening the box. Who was the sender? I certainly wasn't going to wear it, not knowing where it came from, so I went into my bedroom and dropped it in a dresser drawer. Maybe if I waited long enough, the giver would ask me about it.

After a few weeks had passed, no one mentioned the gift and I didn't think much about it. I had narrowed it down to one or two people, both of whom live out of state. I knew both personally and played *Words* with them. I didn't want to ask "oh, by the way, did you send me a gift lately?" The more time that went by, the more awkward that question became, so my gift just stayed in the drawer in my bedroom.

Chapter 10

MONDAY - CAN'T TRUST THAT DAY

My favorite day of the week is Monday. I think of it as my day off. Often, I have work during the weekend, so I usually leave Monday free. This isn't common knowledge; the ladies I work for assume I'm all scheduled up. It's a secret that helps me get things done and stay sane and organized. It is one day I don't have to rush out the door, but I leave an hour in between for my good friend Susan. Brad goes in late on Mondays and usually drops in on his way to work for a cup of coffee and a chat. Sometimes, he brings his laptop with him and gets a head start on his day. It's just part of a routine that might seem boring to someone else. If I want to hang out in my sweats and not dry my hair after my shower, it is okay, Brad is easy to please. We do sound old and married sometimes, or at least it feels that way.

The first thing in the morning I expect a few dozen texts from Susan because we have that standing lunch date. Susan can't do anything without texts flying back and forth to get all her plans crystal clear. Sometimes, I wonder if a phone call wouldn't suffice? Oh well, I guess you have to say it's her style.

This Monday, she had not yet texted and I was just about to jump in the shower. There was a little chill in the apartment on this morning. This old place doesn't have the best insulation and the beach weather can certainly be felt on gray mornings. I had thrown on a pair of old sweats, you know the kind, draw string waist, baggy butt, very unbecoming, topped with an oversized sleep shirt that I had snagged out of Brad's give-away pile. My hair is wadded up on my head with one of those clippy things and I didn't care because I was thinking about dropping in to see the hairdresser today. I had not started the coffee because I figured I had a good forty-five minutes before Brad would show up. It was just a habit of mine to go over to the door and peek out to check the weather - early fog, but it looked like it would clear up. Sunny skies were in the forecast. Perhaps I could even squeeze in a jog on the beach a little later. Bob was in my hand and I purposely set him down on the small second-hand table next to the door. The table was one of those great garage sale finds that worked perfectly to throw the keys and phone on as I came in the door. I decided to leave Bob there, so I wouldn't have to listen to Susan's texting alert that was sure to start while I was in the shower. This morning she would just have to wait. I unlocked the front door just in case Brad got here early while I was in the shower. Brad did have a key, but I thought I would save him the trouble and leave it open. He would probably give me the friendly lecture about keeping it locked and keeping safe. Sometimes, his big city growing up showed. He sometimes forgets how laid back this town is. If he got here early, he could start the coffee. It's one thing he was kind of particular about, he liked it just so. I could do it, but he did it better.

On my way to the shower, I was reminded about this nagging cough I had and went back to give the pharmacy a call to get my prescription filled. I assumed the pharmacist wouldn't be in yet, but I could leave a message and get it later today. The pharmacy is owned by Jack and it's called Jack's Pharmacy. He's great; he treats everyone like an old friend. It always takes me back in time when I walk in because it's been the same for fifty years. The pharmacy is quaint, small, bursting at the seams with one of everything - and Jack knew just where to find everything. It has a real small-town feel. Even though I rarely get sick or need anything, he always remembers me by name. Jack I'm guessing is in his seventies, white hair and real friendly, even flirty, but not in a creepy way. He always says I'm his best-looking customer, but I've heard him say that to the lady in front of me and the lady in the line behind me as well. Everyone just loves Jack. He was getting in early when I called and told me he'd have my prescription filled within the hour. I told him I'd see him in about that long. That was pushing it because I still had to shower, spend time with Brad and text Susan, but that's just what came out.

I set Bob back down on the small table and headed to the bath, through the living room and then the bedroom. I had just touched the bathroom door, when I heard my front door open. Darn, I really did look a mess and wished of all mornings that Brad wasn't quite so early.

"Hey Brad?"

There was no answer. I peeked my head around the partially opened bedroom door. Plan "B" was in my head, I would just throw something a bit nicer on, shake out my hair and put off the shower until after he left. He never stayed more than half an hour and I would rather spend the time with him. Those thoughts barely rushed through my mind because in the next instant, I was sucking in air with nothing coming out of my mouth, but a gasp. Finally, I found the words.

"Who are you?" and then "What are you doing in my apartment?"

It was not Brad that was for sure. This had to be some sort of terrible mistake; probably the guy had accidently walked in the wrong door. My hands instinctively flew up over my head in an effort to shoo him away and it wasn't working. He had a sneer on his face and he gave the door a back kick with his booted foot, it slammed shut and I heard the click of the lock. Now, he was moving closer and I felt as if I was glued to the floor. I knew I was in real trouble.

This guy was large; burly would be the best descriptive word. In two large strides, he had crossed the room and was in my face. Then in one quick move, his rather large hand was over my mouth. I felt like this was an episode of 20/20 and those things never turned out well. His other hand was behind his back and he dropped a large shopping bag to the floor, still keeping a grasp on my face. I then saw it for the first time, a flash of silver - a very large gun. Now, personally I haven't seen many guns up close, so I am not an expert by any means, but I was pretty sure it was real, and I was not in any position to question if it was or not. Then he spoke in a very slow low tone, almost a whisper,

"Good morning Di, how are you doing this morning?"

Who is this guy and is he kidding? I am not doing too well, and I couldn't answer you if I wanted to, with your big hand covering my mouth. How does he know my name?

"Now, I'm going to take my hand off your mouth and you are going to be real quiet, right? I think the walls here could be a little thin and I have *this* and it could make so much noise. We wouldn't want to wake up the whole neighborhood, would we?"

Unable to speak, I just was shaking my head with all the appropriate answers. He didn't seem to be loosening his grip and he kept talking.

"Now, we're just going to take care of some unfinished business, you know?"

What on earth is this guy talking about? His grip loosened, and I felt his hand very slowly come off my mouth. I was very aware that if I started to yell, it could be slapped right back on, so I had to get control somehow of this situation.

Think Diane, think. I needed to figure out what this maniac wanted from me, and what was our 'business' that he was referring to? I wanted Brad to walk in and stop this whole thing, but no, I didn't want him to come in and be in danger too. Did Kaye see this guy come up the walk and snoop around to find out why he is here instead of Brad? Or did she not even look assuming it was Brad's usual Monday morning routine? That would be one good reason why we shouldn't be so predictable and boring – too late to think about that now.

Now, he was pushing me towards my kitchen table, it's a small table for two with two chairs half in the living room and half in the kitchen. I'm not one to do entertaining and usually eat in front of the TV, so we rarely use it. Then he sat me down hard in one of the chairs - I guess I'm using it today.

Grabbing his bag and still holding me and the gun, he fished out a roll of duct tape. It was like the guy had too many hands doing all this and still holding on to me. It didn't help that he was about three times my size. He began to rip off pieces of the tape with his teeth and place them on the table and then he used the first piece to put over my mouth. I'm sure he did this because I looked like a scream was going to burst out of me. Then he taped my right arm to the chair arm and my ankles together. I wasn't going anywhere. He gently placed the gun on the table, but out of my reach and what would I do with it even if I could reach it. Sheer terror was taking me over and my mind was racing. This is the kind of thing you only hear about and never expect it to happen to you. I knew I had to think clearly. I tried to check the time with a casual glance to the clock. Brad normally gets here around, nine to nine fifteen. It's now eight forty-five. Still trying not to be obvious, I glanced at Bob sitting on the table, knowing full well that it was only a matter of time until Susan or someone would call. The stranger's back was to the phone, which seemed to be a plus, but it was making me nervous.

Please don't call me now. Bob, I need you, but I need you to be quiet right now.

"So now, let's chat."

How could I do that with duct tape on my mouth? I was pretty certain he was going to do the talking and I was expected to listen.

He picked up the bag and pulled out a familiar brown/maroon looking box. My mind drifted back to hot summer days at my Aunt's house in Texas, the box was a game of Scrabble. For one quick minute, I thought I would pass out, but I forced myself to blink and focus. Things were now starting to gel. Chat…scrabble…a stranger in my living room who knows my name. Could this be my *Words With Friends* new friend *KILLERWORD*? The name Killer took on a new meaning especially since he had a gun. The queasy feeling returned. He began to speak again, calm almost soft spoken.

"So, let's see how good you really are. I don't like to lose, but then again you don't either, right?"

Once again I was shaking my head in response to his questions. Is this really all this guy wanted? Was he THAT upset with defeat? Well, I'm sure I could play to lose, no problem. I'm not very good at this game on a board where your opponent can see every move you make. When you play *Words With Friends*, you can move words around without anyone knowing. Again, he spoke,

"Sometimes when I play, I like to have a little conversation with myself, you know kind of talking my way through the play. If I was to take off the tape, would you promise to be quiet? Do you think we could do that?"

I responded with a nod.

As he spoke, he was setting up the game. First, he placed the wooden tray to hold the tiles in front of me, and he carefully placed seven tiles on it. Then he did the same on his side of the board. He carefully straightened the board, which struck me as methodical and odd. Considering the predicament I was in, straightening things didn't seem all that important. In an effort to calm myself, I tried to think of something to distract me from reality. My mind wandered to those nifty wooden turn tables that were called Lazy Susan's that you put the game on and turned the game, so it always faces the player. The Lazy Susan only made me think of my friend Susan...please Susan, don't text me now. I glanced at Bob, franticly wondering, how could I get my hands on Bob? I was doing everything I could think of to compose myself.

I couldn't focus on the tiles and suddenly, he shoved back his chair and leaned over to me. In one quick jerk, he ripped the tape off my mouth. My upper lip was on fire and I was pretty sure I'd never have to wax it again, ever.

"So, you like me to go first, right? You always passed to me and made me go first. Did you know I really didn't like that? When you did that, it really bugged me, but you know what, I'm such a nice guy, we are going to play it just like you like to play."

Then he began to think and mumble and tap the gun on his head. This is totally crazy, who would do that? I limited myself to utter only quiet, one-word responses, hoping not to anger this man across the table with a gun. But then I got a little risky.

"So what do you want me to call you - Killer?" I asked.

This brought a roar of laughter that really caught me off guard.

"You are really a smart one aren't you - and cute too."

This was one compliment that I could have done without. With no cheating involved, he proceeded to put down his first, very high point word. I might add I didn't know for sure that it was legitimate, but I certainly wasn't going to challenge him. Next, he requested a piece of paper to write done his points. All I could think of was the notepad and pen on the little table, right next to Bob. I needed to change the subject and get his mind off the paper and my turn. In an attempt to distract him, I tried to flatter him about what a really good word he had just played.

"Yes, it is Di and I have a lot more good words right up here,"

While he talked, he kept tapping the gun against the temple of his head. Now I got to thinking to myself maybe, just maybe, this big shiny gun wasn't even loaded. After all, a person would have to be a real idiot to tap their head with a loaded gun. Which brings me to another related subject. Pistol whipping - what exactly is that? I've heard of pistol whipping, but for the first time in my life, I began to formulate a picture in my mind of what it might be. I had to shake my head and blink myself into clear thinking, this guy needs a word. He started that laughing again.

"Come on Di, you can't lose if you don't play."

Under my breath, very quietly I replied, *"It's Diane."*

For some reason, it just didn't seem right to be called Di by a guy named Killer.

Killer had ever so neatly placed the tiles down, then slowly turned the board to face me. I looked at my letters: E, Y, T, G, I, I, and M. I see absolutely nothing. Maybe I could claim I can't play with my left hand. I'm grasping for straws and feeling the need to chat, just so he doesn't start rummaging around for paper. I deliberately looked past him to the clock on the wall and he turns to look at it.

''Are you taking medicine or something?''

"It's just that my boyfriend will be here real soon," I replied.

I tried to sound casual as I looked back at the clock and then lowering my eyes to the game. His demeanor changed immediately.

"Your what? You have a boyfriend?"

It wasn't like I ever chatted with him any personal information or that he had even asked me anything like that for that matter. I could have been married or fat or old, for all he knew. Good grief, we weren't on a dating site. Then I started to wonder, had he been stalking me in some way and gathering information? Was it even possible for someone to get information about me like that? Then he asked if I am just playing with him about the boyfriend thing. What did he think - that I was going to be his girlfriend now? I couldn't tell if I was making matters better or worse, but I was stalling in a way until I could think of something better to do.

"Yes, I have a boyfriend named Brad, and he'll be showing up here soon."

Suddenly he was out of his chair with a jerk.

I was filled with mixed emotions at his next statement,

"Then we're out of here - change of plans."

At least I didn't have to make a word or worry anymore about him keeping score, but I was anxious about the "change of plans." Next, he started yelling at me that I needed a coat. I hesitated for a minute, both wondering why I needed one and if I even have one. I rarely wear a coat at all, but way back in the hall closet, in the very back, is a black car coat that I have taken to the mountains on occasions. I was still taped up, so I couldn't get it. I described to him where it was. I was thinking as he was rummaging through the closet that it was a good thing I didn't lie to him that I am married because he would probably notice my husband had no clothes in the closet. The coat is oversized and had huge pockets on each side and I started to hatch a plan to get Bob in my pocket on the way out. I couldn't leave Bob here.

Now he must remove this tape and for some reason, being on the move sounded better to me than having to deal with him here. I was so scared that Susan would call or Brad would come in. Who knows what might happen. He didn't seem too happy about me having a real boyfriend.

He started digging in his bag again and brought out a pair of scissors. Finally, he cut through the tape and released me. Now, he pulled me out of the chair and started dragging me towards the bedroom. Major panic on my part caused me to resist, but he stops and yells,

"Shoes, you need shoes."

This was a thoughtful gesture on his part because I was barefooted. As we got to the closet I passed right over all the sandals and flats and went straight for the tennis shoes. He became pushy and tried to hurry things up.

"Come on, come on!"

The tennis shoes were going to take me longer to lace up, but I might get a chance to run and I wanted to be prepared. I've been known to take a jog on the beach and I'm not a bad runner. I was thinking I could outrun this big lug, but the thought of that pistol kept me in check. If I run away, he could shoot me in the back. I needed to be more clever than him. Is that possible?

Now Killer was half-dragging me toward the door with me in my jogging shoes, sweats and wearing a huge black coat. But then something worked for me that was unexpected. As Killer was rushing me to the door, fumbling with the lock, he took his eyes off me for a split second. I was able to slip my hand right over Bob and drop him into my big coat pocket. He sank right down to the bottom of my pocket and Killer never noticed. Thank you Bob, I need you, now please stay quiet until I can mute you. If a call or text or annoying game sound comes in, we are dead. I really needed a distraction.

Killer was mumbling and grumbling under his breath as if he really didn't want to drag me around. Obviously this wasn't his plan. Something else that I figured wasn't in his plan was Kaye, and we were almost to her door. Sure enough, the blue front door of unit #1 popped open and Kaye's little grey head peeked out. All I could think was how wonderful to have such a thoughtful, alert, nosey neighbor. She looked rather confused, probably expecting to see Brad's slim six foot frame standing next to me. Killer stopped dead in his tracks and looked a bit startled, but quickly composed himself.

"Well, who's this?"

It's just like Kaye to get right to the point. I jumped right in feeling like this could be an opportunity that I didn't want to miss. I started by lying about everything I could think of to lie about.

"Oh… Kaye, I'm glad to see you; this is my older brother Dave. He's visited before but I don't think you have ever met him."

I was trying not to stammer and I was definitely talking too fast, but hoping that Kaye would notice. As I was just getting on a roll to drag this conversation out, I was reminded of the danger I was really in. The false hug of his arm turned into the hard, metallic muzzle of a pistol pressing against my back. As frightened as I was, I reasoned, what would he do right here on my walkway in front of a witness? I continued to babble, hoping that Kaye would surely pick up on something. Kaye just looked fascinated with Dave, almost ignoring me.

"Yes, Dave lives in Santa Barbara, right Dave? You still live in Santa Barbara, don't you?"

Not even waiting for an answer, I continued.

"Well, for years, Dave lived in…." and I started to say Atlanta but the gun pressed harder against my back and I just couldn't. There was a pause and I groped for another city – I think I said Ventura. "Gotta' run Kaye, we'll talk later this afternoon."

I never say that to Kaye. We hurried on along the walkway to the street and I turned back and gave her a little halfhearted wave.

73

"That was terrible Miss Di, just horrible. Couldn't you do a little better than that?"

In just a whisper, I corrected him again,

"My name is Diane."

And yes, I know he is right, I could do better. I must do better than that.

My street is less than a block from the main highway and he steered me in that direction, with his arm around me. If anyone had seen us, I'm sure they would have thought we looked pretty odd, me with my hair still wadded up on my head and wearing a heavy winter coat. To my dismay, no one seemed to be out and about and the few people that were, didn't look our way. Normally, this place would be swarming with people, but not today.

Almost the moment we turned the corner, I was surprised to see something that made my heart nearly stop. Right there, parked on Coast Highway, was a huge white semi-truck and trailer. Oh this is great, I thought to myself, I'm taking a ride in a big rig, going who knows where, with an angry, armed Scrabble player. Now all I could think about was getting the phone at the bottom of my pocket turned to silent.

Like a real gentleman, my captor opened the passenger door and literally, physically hoisted me into the cab of the truck. The thing was so far off the ground I would need a step stool to do it myself, but then again, he probably wasn't in the habit of carrying around a female passenger. On second thought, for all I knew, maybe he had done this before. I had to shake that thought from my mind.

In the process of getting in, I managed to shove my hand in my pocket and hold onto Bob. I figured in the time it took him to go around and get in, I could mute him. The flash of metal was quick but I saw it just for a second as he shoved it into an inside pocket of his light-weight jacket.

"Now we know where this is and we know what it can do," he said giving his chest a pat. "It would be very stupid of you to try to get out of here while I walk around to get in."

He was leaning in so close, I could feel his breath as he stood by the side of the cab. Then Killer decided he really didn't trust me and got out another piece of duct tape and wrapped my ankles together. I was grateful he didn't bind my hands, but he was in a hurry and his main concern was me running. I gazed out at the beach on my right. As far as I could see, sand and beautiful aqua blue ocean. How I wanted to jump and run. I looked down and decided I'd probably kill myself trying to jump out of this truck. Then, he put his finger up in the air and gave his chest another pat.

"Remember?" He said, raising his bushy eyebrows.

I just shook my head in response and like lightning, pulled Bob out to mute him, as the passenger door slammed shut. The door was big and solid and made me feel I was now in prison. I watched him watching me as he went around the front, the rig was so high I could just see his head and that was good cover for me as I fumbled with Bob and muted him just as a call was coming in. I couldn't risk looking down to see who was calling. Fortunately, the truck cab is so air-tight he didn't hear Bob ring. Quickly, I pushed Bob back into my pocket. At the same time the driver's side door swung open and Killer climbed up into the driver's seat. Then he pulled the gun out of his jacket pocket and laid it very gently on the floor board right by his foot. This is crazy I thought; who would put a loaded gun on the floor of their truck? This guy must be crazy. Again, I got this flash of a hopeful thought that maybe he's all bluff and this gun wasn't loaded. The front seat of the truck was huge and sitting next to the passenger door, I felt like a small child in a king-size bed. The facts were looking grim: I was trapped in a huge soon-to-be-moving metal box, traveling with a loose cannon of a man with a pistol. I thought to myself that he was making quite a show of starting his "machine" up. Maybe this big rig made him feel like a big man. He idled the engine for just a minute and then skillfully maneuvered it out into traffic. As he did so, on the opposite side of the road in the oncoming traffic I saw a familiar sight. It was a very brief flash of Brad's new pretty red car; the other woman in our simple relationship. It made my heart sink. In that brief moment, I imagined that he saw me too, but maybe that was wishful thinking. How could he possibly see me way up here in the cab of this big truck? At this point, all I could do was hope. He's such a smart guy. Could he put this all together when he gets to the apartment, sees the Scrabble game, talks to

Kaye and remembers this truck? I was feeling like he is my only hope but deep down, I knew that right now this was all up to me. I had to come up with some kind of a plan.

Here's what I had noticed at this point about Killer: he really needed to be in control at all times. He hated it when things didn't go his way, he liked to do most of the talking. My first plan was just talk like crazy, ask him questions, never shut up and maybe he would just want me out of his life and drop me off the first chance he gets. If I was successful, maybe he would drop his whole plan, whatever that might be.

As it turned out, Killer wasn't very appreciative of all my questions, he just grunted instead of answering. My efforts to get him to open up were failing. He did like it however when I asked him how he located me. It seemed like a real ego thing with him. He was so smart to figure it all out. In one of those chats, he explained, when he complained about the snow, I bragged about the good weather in California. I suddenly realized that I told him where I lived, and he simply googled me.

"Since no Di Master came up, I tried Diane Masters and there were only two. The other one was in New York."

Getting back to Bob, he remained in my right hand pocket and I was able to fidget with him a little. I had to be careful because he could be sensitive. My plan was if I could manage to push redial, I could call my last call contact and leave a clue. My last call and only call of the morning was when I called Jack to order my cough medicine. From past experience, I knew that every call went to record after Jack opened in the morning and he caught up at noon. My conversation would have been recorded. I nearly swelled with pride of the genius of remembering this fact and now if I could say the right thing and push the right button, maybe Jack would call Brad about my message.

Killer interjected at about this time that I should really do something about my annoying cough. Believe me, I fully intended to do that and I was glad to know it was bothering him. Brad was the only person who knew I was going to call Jack. Last night when I was coughing, he made me promise to call first thing in the morning. If I knew Brad, he would be following up on everything he could think of to find me. Every time I think about Brad, I feel so bad because I know he was probably frantic.

Now to involve Killer in some kind of meaningful conversation. It needed to be about him. I rambled on about his truck and how great it was and how proud he must be to own it. It seemed to be working because the truck appeared to be a big part of his life.

"What is it that you hauled in this big semi to Los Angeles? It must have been a lot of something to use a truck of this size."

I could tell he really didn't want to answer me and remembered how he complained about playing the game and driving, so maybe there was a common thread with trying to do two things at once. After a rather long pause, he replied.

"Underground furniture."

I truly did not know what he was talking about. I just repeated it in the form of a question.

"Underground furniture?"

80

He sneered his answer out of the corner of his mouth.

"Caskets."

"Yikes, caskets?" I cleared my throat.

"For dead people?"

Killer got a good laugh out of that.

"Yeah, for dead people."

Killer suddenly seemed to enjoy the subject,

"Yep, nice wooden caskets; just delivered a whole big load of them - dozens of them to some place called Rose Hills up by L.A., ever hear of it?"

I had already done a quick count to myself of how many seconds long that message of Jacks was. His message was pretty typical. "I am unable to answer your call, please leave a message or your prescription and I will return your call during this business day. Thank you for your call, Jack's pharmacy." I pushed the proper button on Bob and did the count and then I cleared my throat and loudly and clearly spoke.

"All the way from Atlanta to L.A. with a great big load of

caskets, huh?"

It might not have been the best clue, but it was all I had. If only I had seen some markings on the rig or could relate something to identify it, but I had nothing. Hopefully my message had been sent, now I just needed to stay alive.

Chapter 11

MY LIFE AS A TRUCKER'S LADY

I had been tense for what seemed like hours and doing something constructive, by making the cell phone call, made me feel a little calmer. Being out of ideas and energy, I began to concentrate on the scenery and traffic. I was looking at everything I saw in a new light. It wasn't that I had given up, but I wondered if I would ever see any of these things again. I couldn't get a handle on my emotions and felt very overwhelmed. I kept reminding myself that since I beat this guy at Scrabble, I could win at this game too. Brad and I had talked so much about travel; was this going to be the only trip I would ever have? Not if I could help it.

We seemed to be clipping along at a good speed. I assumed with no load it was faster than with a full load and I knew I was getting further and further from being saved.

I had no idea where we were and I didn't care to ask. This was turning into such a nightmare; my only escape was sleep and so that's what I did. I don't know for how long, it could have been minutes or hours but it was that kind of sleep that you have no power over. When I did awake, it was with a start and I had to remind myself that I couldn't move my legs because they were still taped together. I must have squirmed a little in discomfort and Killer was looking my way when I looked at him. My coat was making me feel hot and uncomfortable, but it was a necessity. I was sweating so much, the cab felt like a sauna. Killer suggested that I take off my coat since we are in the desert and it's hot out there. I told him I'm fine and he replied, "Suit yourself." I will, thank you very much.

I asked a few questions about where we were and where were we going and he said we were about twenty miles from Arizona – which turned out to be the California border town of Blythe. He said he needed to get to Phoenix by late afternoon to pick up a load and then it would be on to Atlanta. I had a sinking feeling that this route covers just about the entire United States. How will Brad ever find me? The discomfort really started to close in on me; I was hungry, I needed to go to the bathroom, I needed a shower. I missed all these things this morning. I was certain this guy was going to kill me and dump me somewhere where no one would ever find me.

One thing I might have going for me is he needs to get to Phoenix. Maybe this will buy me some time.

"There's a rest stop coming up and I need a stretch," he said, pointing ahead.

He is referring to just himself now so I complained and told him I needed to use the ladies room.

The big rig started to slow and we exited to our right to the rest stop. Moving slowly through the rest area, the big rig soon came to a complete stop in a gravel area some distance from the other trucks and cars. I looked out at what I can only describe as an oasis. There were trees and grass and several picnic tables with water fountains in the middle. Most importantly, a building in the middle with restrooms that reminded me - I really need to go.

"This is it," I said to myself. "This is where I get my freedom."

Somehow, I'm going to get away from him. Right here, I told myself. There were a few kids running around after having been cooped up in their cars for hours. I thought back to my childhood, to our long summer family vacations to Texas. It was always a long, boring road trip and we would stop to stretch at places just like this. Mom packed us sandwiches and sodas in a cooler and Dad would sit it on one of those benches. As soon as we were finished eating, my brother and I would run 'amuck' for as long as we could until Dad rounded us up and got us back in the car. It always had to do with keeping on schedule. This was certainly a different circumstance. No happy fun running for me.

The silence really struck me, even with cars whizzing by and children yelling to each other out on the grass. With the engine turned off, everything outside is muffled. I had forgotten how loud the engine is and now, it felt a little eerie.

BRAD SPEAKS

To me this had to be the perfect Monday. Just look at this; the ocean to my left, the sun is peeking out, I can smell the ocean breeze and I don't have a care in the world. I love my Monday mornings with D and I'm reflecting on how glad I am that I moved to California. I could be shoveling snow back east and unhappy with life. I'm so glad that I figured out that wasn't me.

To top it all off, I'm clipping along the Pacific Coast Highway in my brand new car. This is not just a new car, but my very first new car. Oh, it's not a Porsche or some other fancy sports car, but it's mine and it's new. I actually have to breathe in deeply occasionally to get the full effect of that new car smell. Yep, it's not used, it smells new. I've probably gone through about five used cars in my short life of twenty seven years. Don't get me wrong, everyone of them holds a place in my heart, but this one, this one will always be special. This one is in my row of ducks, one of my goals that I have worked hard for. It may sound selfish but hey, a guy needs to have wheels. Besides, it's not just me, I'm thinking about the future, the future with D. She seemed very pleased with it too. I'm thinking of suggesting we take a drive up the coast this weekend and break it in. Today I'm going to suggest that to her and see what she thinks. We haven't had much of a chance to get her out on the road. Around Southern California it's just a lot of looking for a parking space.

Glancing sideways towards the beach, I saw a sight I don't often see, a big rig, headed South, right here on Coast Highway. This is a narrow highway not connected to a freeway and you don't get many large trucks traveling on it. It's a real slow go in the summer with all the tourists. Whoever is driving it has it all shined up. The reflecting glare of the sun nearly blinding. As I'm thinking all this I came right up onto Fourth St. and made my turn toward D's apartment. Just to prove what a perfect day I've got going here, there's a parking space right out front of 1291 Fourth Street – D's apartment. I must be leading a charmed life or something, because this usually never happens. I pulled in carefully not to touch the tires to the curb and left plenty of space behind the car in front of me - can't be too careful, she doesn't have a scratch on her yet.

I reached over and grabbed my laptop on the passenger seat, got out and locked her up. Taking the corner of my shirt, I gently rubbed a little smudge on her already shiny surface then I gave the tire just a little kick, for no particular reason.

I gave her a name - Lola. I got that idea from D and her crazy phone named Bob. The name fits her because she is kind of sexy. I'm not sure if D approves, I thought to myself with a chuckle.

At this point walking up to the apartment and as further proof that I live a charmed life, unit number one's door where nosy Kaye lives didn't open. Wonders never cease. I nearly tripped myself on the walkway as I turned my gaze back at Lola for one last look.

Reaching D's unit, I gave the door one light knock - no sense alerting Kaye of my arrival now. As I touched the door, I noticed it's slightly ajar. I've really got to talk to this girl of mine about her personal safety. I don't care how safe you feel, no one should leave their doors open, and obviously, Kaye is not on duty this morning.

With just a nudge, the door swings open and I was standing in the living room. Stepping in, I called out, "D" and not hearing a thing, I repeated it a little louder the second time. "D?" Still no response. The apartment is dead silent and right away, I noticed there was not the usual smell of coffee in the air. The place is so small, it normally permeates the whole room.

"Hey, D, where are you?"

There are not a lot of places to go, so I edge over towards the bedroom door standing wide open. Then the kitchen table to my right caught my eye. Why on earth and with whom is she playing Scrabble? I didn't even know she owned a Scrabble game. They didn't get very far on this game there is only one word on the board and it sure is a strange word, not one I'm familiar with. I had one quick romantic thought that the board would have a little love note spelled out to me on it, D is like that. Not this time, I guess. I moved closer to the bedroom again, feeling a bit invasive and called out her name again. Then I noticed D's favorite big blue purse sitting right on the bed. A closer look and I saw the bathroom door open also. The bed was made, the room neat, the closet door open. She is not in this apartment and I was feeling very uneasy. There is probably a perfectly logical explanation for this. She probably grabbed a couple of quarters and headed over to the laundry room at the end of the building. I decided to check it out. This is careless and not like her at all, so she must have been in a hurry.

Leaving the apartment I headed up the walkway and around the corner towards the laundry room. It's tiny and has only one washer and one dryer. The room was empty and the appliances were not in use, no swishing of the washer and no humming of the dryer.

Now, I jogged back to number two, although not knowing what to do next. Something was wrong. Really wrong, and I didn't really want to involve Kaye, but there wasn't a choice. Kaye usually knows everything that is going on at any given time. My knock was urgent and the door opened so quickly, she must have been standing right on the other side of it. It actually gave me a start and I jumped back. I started asking questions rapid fire.

"I need to know where my girlfriend is...now!"

Kaye looked baffled that I was being so abrupt and I knew I'd have to apologize for that later. She didn't seem as concerned as I was and explained that Diane had just left a few minutes earlier with her brother, Dave.

"It's a shame you just missed them."

I had never met Dave, but I knew she did have a brother named Dave. Still, D would have called me to say he was here and if she left with him she certainly would have taken her purse. I continued shooting questions at Kaye, knowing that time was of the essence. The most disturbing thing was that Kaye mentioned that Dave lived in Santa Barbara. One thing I did know about Dave was that he lived in Chicago and that's a far cry from Santa Barbara.

"Who said Dave lived in Santa Barbara, D or her brother?" I asked.

When she replied that Diane made it a point to tell her that her brother lived in Santa Barbara, I was sure D was trying to tell us, "This is not my brother!"

My head was swimming, what to do next? I felt that I should call the police, but I was clinging to the hope that this was just some crazy mix up and I would later feel foolish for being this frantic. I ran out front to the curb and looked both ways, not knowing what I was looking for and I saw absolutely nothing out of the ordinary. Other than the way the apartment was left a little carelessly, there was no sign of a struggle and it certainly didn't look like a robbery with her purse on the bed. Her purse! I had not even looked. was anything missing? I rushed in and dumped the contents on the bed and picked through the pile. It looked pretty much like a woman's purse looked I guess, not really being sure what I was looking for but then it hit me... no Bob! He wasn't on the table by the door either. I grabbed my phone and quickly pushed her number. Not only did I not get an answer, it just shut off, with no voice mail either. Think Brad, think.

Then it came to me - the cough, the pharmacy. She planned to go to the pharmacy first thing this morning. Could it be as innocent as her brother visiting unexpectedly and then the two of them walking over to the pharmacy? I was again on the move, thinking of all the possible scenarios. I started down the walk in a jog, which escalated into a full run by the time I reached the sidewalk. The pharmacy was literally one block up and one block over and I knew I could get there faster on foot than by car. It was back to that parking problem, anywhere close you could spend more time looking for a parking place than you could, just walking. I made it there in record time and burst through the door of the pharmacy. I'm grateful that the place is empty.

I flew in yelling, "Jack, Jack".

I couldn't see him, but I knew he was there, he always was. Towards the back of the pharmacy was a long tall counter area that you could see only the top of Jacks head. His grey head peeked up from his work and he was grinning from ear to ear.

"Well, look who's here, it's my favorite guy Brad. What's up there Brad? I never see you, that's good. I guess you must be the healthiest guy around."

Usually the small talk was refreshing, but today I just had to cut him off.

"Was Diane in here today and was she alone?"

Jack still wasn't in a hurry and I didn't know how to impress him with the urgency of the situation. He replied that Diane had indeed called earlier that morning just as he was opening up, and she ordered some cough syrup.

"She told me she'd be in within the hour, but she hasn't showed up."

Jack acknowledged that this wasn't like her and he hoped there wasn't anything wrong. Little did he know *everything* was wrong, but I just couldn't alarm him. Or maybe it was too alarming to me. He asked if I would like to take the cough syrup to her and pulled a little white bag out from under the counter,

"She can pay for it later." Jack said with a smile.

Thanking him and running towards the door, Jack said something that changed my hasty exit into a 180 degree spin.

"You know something odd did happen this morning shortly after she called," Jack said, scratching his head.

"Yes Jack, tell me."

I was willing at this point to grab at any straw.

"Well you see, I record all my calls that come in, if I'm busy and can't answer or even if I do answer, just for a record you know. That way, I don't forget or miss anything. The prescriptions are all there for me to review if I need to." He led me back behind the counter to where his answering machine was located, then began to fumble with his machine, going back to the beginning of the day. I was shifting back and forth and my patience was getting real thin, but what if Jack had some information that would help me find Diane. So I stood shifting my weight and fingering the crisp white bag, wishing I could take over myself. Then I heard it, a little muffled at first, almost inaudible. Clearly, I heard Diane's voice.

"All the way from Atlanta to L.A. with caskets."

It sounded so odd, so I asked Jack to play it again. Yes, that's exactly what she said. And it was definitely Diane's voice.

I grabbed a pen off the counter and scribbled on the bag what I heard. I had no idea what it meant or how it would help me. I took off in a run towards the door, yelling back thanks to Jack. The bell that let Jack know he had a customer, rang on my way out and the door slammed behind me; I was in a full run. I was headed toward the apartment, but I had no idea why. I pulled out my cell phone and dialed 911.

By the time I entered the apartment, I could barely breathe. Running my hand through my hair, I started wondering what I would tell the police when they arrived. Where would I start; how would I explain this story; would they believe me? I was fully aware the boyfriend or husband always came under scrutiny. Now I was thinking such dark thoughts. No, this couldn't be happening. Any minute now, Di would be walking in the door, wondering what all the fuss was about. I would scold her for leaving things the way she did and hug her real tight and then we would go on being the couple that lives here in this beautiful town and enjoy being together.

Two nice policemen arrived in less than a half hour. I still did not know what to say or where to start. When I say nice, they were almost too nice, almost condescending in

97

the manner they questioned me. Their questions were perfunctory, almost simplistic: What is my relationship to Diane? When was the last time I saw her? Had anything like this ever happened before? I just answered questions and didn't volunteer anything extra. Telling them she never had a Scrabble board out on the table just sounded like a detail they wouldn't know what to think of. They gave me their cards and we exchanged numbers. I could call back later and file a report if she was truly missing. She was not, as of this morning, considered missing. I expected this response, but my heart sank anyway. I just thought this would be an exception. Their attitude was that it was going to be a beautiful day and she had probably gone out to take a jog on the beach. I was jumping out of my skin. 'Forget you. I will find D myself before anyone files a stupid report,' I thought. I didn't say it out loud because I didn't want to be the jerk boyfriend, but I knew it was a fact. I WOULD find her today and she WOULD be OK!

ATLANTA, GEORGIA

The biggest clue of all came to me just about the time the squad car pulled away from the curb. The weird Scrabble guy is from Atlanta; Killer Word, the truck driver is from Atlanta. It sounded like such a stretch, but could something that strange be happening? I quickly reached for the pharmacy bag and reread my own writing: Caskets from Atlanta to L.A.

My laptop was out and the search started. Then I remembered the semi-truck traveling on crowded Coast Highway earlier that morning. Wow, I may have just missed D and her brother. No, I just missed D and Killer. That thought sickened me. Who is this guy?

I grabbed my laptop and googled casket makers in Georgia. Sure enough, there are a lot of them. Now there's something I never would have even thought about: where are caskets made? There seems to be at least three of them in the Atlanta area and this is where I need to start.

I called the first one listed: Abbott's Casket Manufacturing. I needed to know if they had recently sent a shipment to L.A. Absolutely nothing is more frustrating than to have a real mission to accomplish and getting nothing but voice mail, but that is what happened. I tried to leave a brief message that didn't make me sound like a maniac. I didn't let it deter me however and went right to the next one – Peacock & Green Casket Company. After one quick ring, the voice of a Southern Belle, dripping with honey answered the phone. The tone of her voice was ready to sooth the caller who had just lost a loved one in death.

"Why no, we're a very small factory and we make a very limited number of one of a kind elegantly carved and embellished caskets. They are mostly bought locally, but we do have a catalog of prices and examples of our work. Let me get your address and I'll send it out right away".

Bless her heart, as they say in the South, she is probably their number one sales person. She obviously didn't have a clue about what I needed, and I really hated to hang up on her, but it was on to the next.

Number three was Langmore Caskets Inc. and their phone is answered with a not-so-friendly male voice. I got the impression my call was a bother to him.

"Was I a buyer, did I have a shipping problem, what did I need?"

I slowly told him I was really sorry to bother him, but I really needed some information and this was a matter of life or death. He actually laughed at that phrasing, which even I have to admit, was really inappropriate.

"Yeah, I hear that a lot Buddy, after all we are talkin' about caskets here."

O.K. so that wasn't the best thing to say and I didn't want to waste any more time, so once again I explained myself, trying not to get too detailed. What I needed to know was if, say in the last day or two, had they shipped any caskets to the Los Angeles area?

"Ah, sure we sent out a shipment to Rose Hills, that's one of our big accounts in California."

Now I'm getting somewhere. He continues,

"You guys must be dropping like flies out there, we sent a whopping three dozen your way."

I could ignore his attempt at comedy, I was getting needed information. So, trying to keep my excitement in tow, I asked,

"Who's your driver?"

"Wait a minute Buddy, we just make them here, we don't drive around with them."

So I continued to ask questions, but I could tell that I am wearing thin with this guy and I needed more from him. He starts in,

"Well sometimes these things get sent out by rail, and we even crate them up and ship them by boat."

I'm losing him now and needed to pull him back.

"but this load to L.A. went in a big semi truck, right?"

He's mumbling now and I can tell he's flipping pages trying to get me an answer. He mutters under his breath about how unreliable these trucking companies are and how they rarely get stuff delivered on time and then it ends up being his fault. I continue to let him rant and then he pops up with 'Adams Brothers trucking',

"Yep. That's it, Adams Brothers. Just a small company, three brothers, pretty good guys, haven't had any real complaints about them. They each own their own rigs and run a pretty tight business."

Great, so I ask which one of the brothers drove to L.A.

"Hmm. That I couldn't tell you. Someone here just called the company and placed an order and they took care of the rest. Hell, I don't care which one drives as long as they get them there on time."

I'm pushing it here, but I keep going,

"So would that "someone" you mentioned that took the order know?"

He heaves a big sigh, but agrees to transfer me over to the "gal" who probably would have scheduled the shipment. I looked at my watch - time is really flying and D is getting further and further away from me. Now I paced around the room waiting for a transfer, my nerves were on edge, but I felt I was making a little progress. It was better than sitting and waiting for Diane to become an official "missing person."

I nervously ran my fingers through my hair so much that I was about to tear it out.

While I wait for "someone" to come on the phone, I begin to really look around the room to see if there is anything out of place that I might have missed. Everything looked neat and pretty much like it usually did. D was one to keep the place neat and tidy. The only thing that stuck out as wrong was the Scrabble game on the table with that one word on the board. As I crossed the room, something very small and silver caught my eye under the table. I had to get down on my hands and knees to retrieve it and recognized it right away as a small piece of duct tape. I'm positive that D doesn't own a roll of duct tape - that was a guy thing. I, on the other hand, have the stuff everywhere and I'm thinking to myself that this could be a bad sign – something I don't want to think about right now.

The "gal" finally came on the line, friendly and cheerful but didn't have a clue about what I wanted. I sat down on the kitchen chair and slowly and deliberately explained the reason for my call. If I went too fast, it seemed to confuse her. She seemed sweet, but not what you'd call attentive. I needed to know whatever she could tell me about the most recent California delivery to Rose Hills Cemetery. Did she know which one of the Adams brothers drove the shipment? Now, she got chatty and wanted me to know that she didn't think much of the brothers. She thought they were very disrespectful to her and didn't respect women in general. This was all good to know I guess, but it wasn't helping me find Diane. I was starting to form a picture of these guys and I was getting angrier because I am sure one of them has my girlfriend. Showing as much respect as I could muster and trying not to rush or hurry her, I asked her name, just to show her I was not like the Adams brothers. She replied, Gloria, and I said her name every time I spoke, just hoping she would take that as a sign that I cared.

"So, Gloria, can you remember which Adams brother you spoke to and which one was to make the delivery?"

I didn't want to be condescending, but she seemed childlike and really needed things to be spelled out. She went on to explain there was one named Bud who usually answered the phone and did the scheduling, and then either

Greg or Don did most of the driving. She was expounding details now that sounded more like her opinion than fact. She thought that Bud didn't like long hauls and delivered more locally because she knew they all had a rig but had never seen him in person. Once again, I pressed her,

"Gloria can you tell me who drove?"

I felt like I was on the cusp of getting a name which seemed important, but I hadn't yet thought of what I'd do with the name when I got it. I heard that shuffling of papers and knew this girl was all heart and was making a real effort to help me, but then came her reply,

"I'm really sorry sir, but I never asked and Bud never told me who would actually do the delivery."

The only thing I could do was ask for the number of Adams Brothers Trucking and Gloria did just that, she gave me the number and wished me good luck in getting answers to my questions. I felt like I'd made a friend, but I also felt very disappointed.

Now, I had to cook up a real good reason to call Bud Adams. I also had the information that the delivery was made to Rose Hills. Somehow, I wondered if I should call them first because I would have to be so careful making that call to Georgia. I googled Rose Hills Cemetery and noted that they had a couple of locations in the L.A. area. Each location had several numbers, so I started at the top and worked my way down, this could take some time, which really worried me. Of course, I got the recorded message first with choices depending what department is needed. 'Pre-need' I assumed was if you weren't dead yet, the remaining numbers, and there were many, had to do with every aspect of the cemetery: location, hours of visitation etc. etc. No choice came even close to 'where do you get your caskets from and who delivers them?' I needed a real live person. Maybe I should start with 'pre-need' because after all - I am in need.

Several rings later a woman with a pleasant voice came on the line, but she had no idea where the caskets came from or where they were kept, let alone who got them there. They did however have a showroom and she would be more than happy to make an appointment with me, so I could pick out the one I liked. She sounded a bit like a used car salesman and I found myself hoping I wouldn't be looking to pick one out. Once again, I was veering off onto the wrong road.

"Listen, I don't want to be rude, but I have reason to believe my girlfriend was abducted by a guy who delivered a shipment of caskets to your cemetery".

"Oh dear, oh my, that's terrible, have you called the police?" She gasped.

I was getting nowhere, and the clock was ticking. She offered to transfer me to the showroom. Maybe someone over there knew something that would be helpful to me. After what turned out to be three transfers, I got this business-sounding voice that tells me I need to call such and such a number and they would be able to get me over to the warehouse manager - where the caskets are actually housed. Now just when I think I'm getting somewhere, a recording puts me through to voice mail and the message is for me to leave my number and they will return my call within one business day. It was becoming clear that if you were not dead, they were not interested.

Running out of options, It was time for me to call Bud Adams in Atlanta Georgia.

THE REST STOP

Killer parked the truck on a gravel area as far away as possible from the other trucks and vehicles at the rest stop. After a quick scan of the stop, I counted maybe ten other big rigs and six or seven cars. Surely, someone here could help me. Killer opened his door and jumped to the ground. He looked me right in the eye, so as to say "don't do anything stupid." No gun on the floorboard, so I knew it was back in his waistband. He slammed the door and moved himself in front of the cab facing me, making sure I am in full view. With his arms over his head and hands locked, he stretched and pulled and then dropped his arms behind his back and stretched some more, then he swung his whole body around and shook it out. I am real glad he loosened up, after all I'm the one who had been sitting in one position with my ankles taped up for hours. He started to wander a little way from the truck, but still in my sight with one eye on me the whole time. He then wandered

109

over to another driver to chat for a minute. I couldn't tell if he knew this guy or if he is just talking to a stranger. I wondered what would happen if I should stomp my feet and yell or bang on the window, but again I remembered the fact that the gun is not on the floor and probably on him. Just about the time I have that thought, Killer winks at me and pats his waistband just a little. I decide to get Bob out knowing that the worst thing that could happen would be to get caught doing it. He would probably throw Bob as far as he could right here at this rest stop and I'd never see him again. As if he could read my mind that I was up to something, he fairly sprinted to my door and flung it open. My hand was in my pocket and holding Bob, but I just let him slide back to the bottom of the deep pocket again.

"You need to go to the little girl's room I suppose?"

He says this lightly like we are such good friends out on a nice Monday drive. He fills me in on his chat that he apparently had made up a story with the trucker "friend" that I am his girlfriend making a run with him and that I have been a little under the weather. He got him to get his "trucker lady" to come over to help out. He hurried to get the duct tape off my ankles before she got to us. She agreed to accompany me to the restroom, just in case I passed out. So, he once again physically got me down and out of the cab and as I touched down, right on cue, here came the trucker lady. Not being able to move my feet around for who knows how many hours, I felt wobbly and had trouble walking, which gave him the perfect opportunity to affectionately put his arm around me to steady me. The trucker lady was exactly what I would imagine a trucker lady to be. She looked a bit worn and probably not as old as the age I would guess she was. Even though rough looking, she gave me a smile and I could tell she had a heart by the expression on her face. She rushed to my other side to support me and introduced herself as Mabes. Under normal circumstances, the name would be cause for conversation, but I said nothing. Killer filled in for me as if I'm a mute and tells her I am Diane, his girlfriend. I find it amusing that for the first time on this whole adventure, I am finally Diane.

In a rough, smoker's voice, Mabes asked,

"Honey, are you OK?"

I just shake my head and throw in a cough for good measure. It comes to me that Killer has set up this restroom break like a Scrabble play.

"Now Di, I'm going to walk you right over to the restroom and Mabes will stand right at the entrance, so she can hear you if you need help. I'll be right around the corner and if Mabes gives me the word, I'll come in to help, you know if you think you're going to faint or something."

Then he asks Mabes to run on ahead and check out the restroom and just make sure no one is in our way. Mabes ran ahead and did just what she was told to do. It was the most complicated and crazy set of plans to keep me in line and I was amazed that he threw it all together in such a snap. With Mabes out of earshot, Killer jerks me hard towards him and whispers in my ear,

"Nothing stupid right? If you say anything, I'll kill both of you," patting his chest. "I mean what I'm saying, I need to be able to trust you. I will have my eyes on Mabes and she will have her eyes on you. You mess up and this nice lady that's helping is in trouble too. Do you understand?"

I understand perfectly. This guy was getting worse - this was his first real threat to my life. Killer meant business, we are not out on a joy ride. What does he really want with me? That comment about trust really throws me and it occurs to me that he thinks we have a real relationship.

I was walking fine at this point and I was able to shake off the stiffness and if not for the tight grip on my arm, I might have considered trying out my running shoes. He walked me all the way up to the restroom. It didn't have a door, just a long tunnel entrance and standing there, like my personal valet was Mabes. She took over walking me the rest of the way, then said the very thing I dreaded most.

"Here honey, let me take your coat."

It's not like I would be able to make a call once I got in the stall of the restroom, but the anxiety of losing Bob became overwhelming.

Before I can protest, she slipped it off and folded it over her arm. Killer added his two cents as he sees her with my bulky coat, saying that I must have been having chills to be able to wear that thing all day. I could hear their voices bouncing off the walls. I followed the plan: I went, I made it quick, I washed my hands with no soap available, I splashed cold water on my face and air dried my hands by waving them back and forth and I was out of there. On my way out, I picked up a corner of Brads shirt to dry my face and the smell of the shirt made me choke up a little; half a cry and half a cough, then I quickly composed myself.

"Her cough sounds pretty nasty," Mabes commented to Killer, speaking right over me like I wasn't there. Killer replied in a loving boyfriend tone,

"Yeah we've got to get this little gal back to Phoenix and to the doctor."

He thanked Mabes and she insisted that it was no problem at all - that's just what one fellow trucker would do for another. He chuckled and gave her a slap across the back, all the while keeping a firm grip on my arm. I found myself eyeballing my coat that I desperately wanted back. I felt naked without it and I wanted to reach out and grab it, but I didn't want Killer to think it was important to me. Mabes walked with us towards the truck and the two of them small talked about routes and roads and compared rigs. She finally passed the coat, but not to me. This is great, I thought - now Killer has my coat *and* Bob.

As we got closer to the truck, for the first time, I focused on the small identifying graphics on the door: Adams Brothers Trucking, Atlanta Georgia and some numbers that I knew I would not be able to remember. I wished I had that information earlier, I could have passed it on.

They said their goodbyes and Killer guided me back up into the cab of the truck. For the first time, he looked a little nervous as he scanned the area. There were people milling around and I'm sure he didn't want to be seen whipping out his duct tape. Killer had been very careful in parking his rig where my door wasn't exposed to view. In my mind, I wondered if he had done something like this before and that thought gave me the chills. That would make him a professional what? Serial killer? Why does he call himself Killer anyway? I literally shake myself back to the here and now.

What to do next? I heard the noise of tape ripping and in his rush, he got rougher tying me up this time. All these things are falling in on me; I was about to leave a place I thought might be my opportunity for escape. He has now officially threatened my life, and now I haven't got Bob with me. The side door slammed again. I started looking frantically for a face to connect with - but there was no one in view. He crossed in front of me slinging my coat over his shoulder. In one quick motion, he is in the driver's side seat and he proceeds to throw my coat over into the space behind his seat. I imagined Bob getting hurt in the fall.

"Now that was real good, you didn't cause any trouble,"

Killer praised me and reached over to pat my shoulder. My natural reflex kicked in and my shoulder recoiled at his touch. I immediately had a second thought that maybe I should hide my feelings and not anger him. What I didn't need is an angry guy with a gun driving me off into the sunset.

What I did need is Bob, how did I let that happen? We were in the desert and asking for my big winter coat was probably not a smart thing to do. Maybe I could get it back at night. Maybe I could ask him if I could use it as a pillow. Thinking about night time is one more scary thought. What is going to happen tonight – where is he taking me?

Once we were back on the road, Killer's demeanor changed, and he seemed more relaxed, almost happy. He seemed pleased with himself like he was playing Scrabble and hitting all the triples.

It's time for me to ask a question that has just been waiting to be asked. I coughed and cleared my throat in preparation, not knowing if this is the right thing to say, but I was starting to wonder if there is a right thing or wrong thing to say.

"So, do you want me to call you Killer or what?"

The silence was heavy in the air and for a minute, I thought he was going to ignore me completely.

"I assume your name is Adams but Killer Adams doesn't sound like a real name, you know what I mean?"

I take a breath,

"So it's just a nickname for some reason or other, huh?"

Still nothing from Killer and he starts to move in his seat

like he needs to get comfortable. Now it's his turn to clear his throat which I assumed meant he was going to speak. He took his time and started out slowly,

"You know what I think? Huh?"

I was afraid to speak and started to wish that I had never started this conversation.

"What I really think is that you ask too many questions. And since this is a Q and A, maybe I should ask you a couple of questions of my own. Like I've been wondering this whole trip why you're not wearing your necklace I got you. Huh? Why aren't you wearing it?"

Now his voice was raised and angry. I realized right away that I needed to defuse this question. I needed to answer it correctly or this guy's going to drive us off the road or something.

I started off as calmly as I could manage, explaining how we left in a hurry, so all I wore were sweats and a t-shirt. If I had time to get ready before we left, I could have put it on. I was lying now, and I know I'm not very good at it, so I was forcing myself to sound sincere. To be honest, I wasn't sure which drawer I had dropped it in, months ago. Then I said that it sure would have helped if I would have known it was from him, after all, there was no return address and no note included. Finally, my little mystery is solved. I should have known all along. Then things start to get sticky when he replied.

"So, what is it with you? Do you have so many admirers that you just could not figure out which one sent it to you?"

This guy not only had a temper but a streak of jealousy too. I needed to be careful what I say because somehow in his sick imagination, he thought we had something going on together. In all his Scrabble chats, there never was a hint of the fact that he admired me. He obviously, along with all his other problems, doesn't do well expressing himself. I tried to pacify him by telling him that I don't have many admirers.

"I thought my girlfriend that I play Words with, who lives in Utah might have sent it – it's cute and looks like something she might have picked out for me," I said.

He finds this amusing and gives me one of his big belly laughs.

"What, you didn't think it was from that boyfriend of yours?"

I felt a little sick in the pit of my stomach knowing that's exactly what I thought when the box came. I continued to lie,

"No, no, I figured it was from you, after all we are the ones playing *Words With Friends* together."

I didn't want him to say another thing about my boyfriend. He had such a nasty way of saying it, so I tried to steer the conversation in another direction.

Come on Diane, what would soothe this guy? He has such an ego, I figured he needed to talk about himself. So, I went for buttering him up. That couldn't hurt.

"What got you interested in *Words* anyway – you must be very educated – you have such an amazing vocabulary."

Sure enough, I struck a chord that got him to talk.

It seems that trucking wasn't exactly a lifelong plan.

Trucking wasn't his chosen profession, but something that came his way when his two brothers decided to buy out this small trucking company and asked him to come on board. He had always liked to drive and get out on the open highway, so he thought why not? Killer, of all things, was an educated man and at one time was a school teacher. I sure wouldn't want this guy teaching any child of mine, but that's what he did. He taught High School English to freshman-aged kids for two years. It seems that he hated every minute of it though. Then came that term again, "He couldn't trust them." If he turned his back for even one minute, he lamented, they were laughing and throwing paper wads at him. The discipline problems with the kids was only half the problem, they just didn't want to learn. If he asked them to do a paper and they did it, he couldn't read it because they couldn't spell. In his second year, he decided to arrange a spelling bee, hoping that at least some of them would enjoy competition and learn something from the few that took it serious. Well, it seemed that plan backfired because they didn't appreciate that either. The kids just used it as an hour to "Goof-off" - as he put it.

121

Killer needed to get this off his chest; the rant went on for miles. I think in miles instead of hours and minutes now because all I can think about is how far away from home I am getting. I don't have a watch because I always used Bob for that, but I can read the billboards by the side of the road that tell you it's six miles to McDonalds and when I see McDonalds, I know we've gone another six miles.

The McDonald's signs made me think of how hungry I was. I never ate breakfast, and I could tell just by the way I felt we were way past noon. I wondered if I should mention it or just wait. Surely at some point, this big guy would get hungry.

Any other Monday, I would have been sitting at some cute little café, eating with Susan. To think that I ever complained. Susan had probably frantically called Brad and I about a million times by now, I thought.

BRAD'S MONDAY

I had started off my Monday like any other Monday and now my world had been turned upside down. Right away, I put a call into work and let my boss know what's going

122

on. He's one of the nicest guys you could ever meet, and was concerned as could be. He told me to do whatever I needed to do and not worry about work at all. He wanted to know if he could do anything and of course, I didn't have a clue what I'm doing, let alone tell someone else what to do. He asked me to keep him posted and just please go out there and find her. Believe me that is what I intended to do.

By 10 am the texts and calls started coming in from Susan. I knew they would because the two of them had their standing lunch date. At first, I ignored the calls because I had no idea what I would tell her, but I was pretty sure I knew how she would react. Susan's O.K. but she's one of those people who can really get on your nerves. She has the tendency to over-react about the smallest of things. I know I couldn't ignore her forever, but I really didn't want to talk to her because it takes up time that I didn't want to waste. Around ten thirty, I went ahead and texted her something brief. I let her know that it doesn't look like Di is going to be around for lunch and I don't know why she is not answering her phone. I tried to keep it light so she didn't flip out on me. I was hoping that I could come up with some logical explanation for her soon.

Not ten minutes went by and there she was, standing on Diane's front step. She wanted to know what was going on and every detail, peppering me with questions. I guess she had the right and I know she was sincere, but somehow speaking about it became very difficult. Thinking is one thing, but when I started vocalizing to Susan what had happened and what I thought, I had to struggle to keep my emotions in check.

My panic somehow helped her to be more logical. She must have known somehow if we both spun out at the same time, we wouldn't get anything done. As much as I didn't want her here, it was becoming evident that I needed somebody. We needed a plan. We needed to get busy doing something constructive. Susan decided she would comb through the apartment and see if we overlooked anything that might be important. Like me, she was very concerned that D's purse was left sitting on the bed. Susan agreed that she wouldn't just go off and leave it. I told her that I had already dumped it out and noticed that Bob wasn't in the purse or anywhere else in the apartment for that matter. The big question was, if she had Bob with her, why is she unable to use him? I tried to keep the duct tape discovery to myself, but when I finally told her, she went into panic mode again. I must be calm, I reminded myself. If we both fall apart, we'll get nowhere.

At least, through all of this, I got the impression that Susan completely trusted me and doesn't suspect I have anything to do with her disappearance. In other words, she didn't ask to go through the contents of my car and look for duct tape. I am grateful for that.

All this activity alerted Kaye that something was going on next door that she didn't know about, and since the door was ajar, she popped her head in. She told us she saw cops earlier and wondered why we are here and Diane isn't. Now *she* needed to be filled in on the events of the day and I really gave her the briefest of explanations. Kaye muttered that she didn't buy that whole brother story because this guy didn't look one bit like Diane. Oh, and by the way Diane never went anywhere looking like such a mess as she did. All I could think is this was a fine time to draw these conclusions after the fact. I just couldn't keep my end of the conversation up and Kaye eventually wandered off, muttering that we could do what we wanted, but she was going to call the police again. I didn't attempt to stop her, there usually was no stopping her anyway.

Susan left us and went back into the bedroom. She was determined to find something that would help and now she was yelling for me to come and look at something. Susan stood in front of the dresser and I could see her in the mirror when I came into the room. She was dangling a chain in front of her and asked me what I thought. To be truthful, I didn't have much of an opinion. At first, it looked like a piece of jewelry and I didn't see any importance in it. As I got closer, I could see that it has a wooden Scrabble tile on it in the shape of the letter D. Well, it certainly wasn't anything that D ever wore and doesn't look like anything she would pick for herself. I was curious as to where it would have come from, but it also didn't seem to be of any help. I picked up and examined the box with the cotton in it. To myself, I think someone must have given it to her, perhaps her captor, but

I didn't share that thought with Susan.

Just then my phone rang. It was Rose Hills returning my call. I repeated what I told them the first time, but to someone new, and they confirmed that they indeed received a delivery from Adams Brothers Trucking. The driver signed the invoice with a scribble and they apologized that they couldn't read the drivers name. I sat down on one of the kitchen chairs, phone in hand and Susan standing over me and began to feel hopeless. What should I do now, twenty-four hours means all day and night and a good part of tomorrow with D just being driven further and further away? I contemplate getting a ticket and flying to Atlanta, but how would that help? How long would it take me to get there? How long would it take them to get there driving?

I grabbed the laptop from where I had tossed it on the couch and moving the kitchen table, I began typing in anything and everything and that I could think of: routes, distances and the times it would take to get there. Susan was trying to help, but she just kept talking, and finally when I couldn't take it anymore, I gave her a task to do, to

127

get her out of my hair.

"Hey, go into D's room in the closet and get her overnight bag. Find whatever you think she might need and put it in, she's going to need some stuff when I find her."

Susan stood frozen, looking at me like I'm a crazy man and I just keep going,

"you know, toothbrush, brush, change of clothes, whatever she might need. Oh, and here put this in too."

I passed the white pharmacy bag with the cough syrup to her.

"D's got a rotten cough, she needs this."

Susan got the point; we both needed to just keep moving forward and doing something positive.

In the middle of my research my phone rang again. It was Adams Brothers Trucking returning my call. The caller identified himself as Bud Adams and he seemed polite - probably thinking he was going to be getting some new business. My mind was spinning, I have to do this right, I reminded myself - I must find out what I need to know while not raising suspicion.

I responded with a big fat lie.

"Yes, this is Jim from Rose Hills Cemetery. I believe that one of your drivers was here earlier with a delivery?"

Bud was obviously annoyed because his tone changed noticeably.

"Yes, we did, is there a problem?"

"No, no not at all, your driver did a wonderful job and I didn't even catch his name."

I'm really vamping for time now.

"You know these caskets are like fine pieces of furniture and you can't just be throwing them around, but your driver showed the merchandise the respect it deserved."

"O.K. I get it, but what is it you need?"

I need a plan and I need it quick, I said to myself.

"Yes your driver, he signed the delivery invoice, but I just can't read it."

I was talking fast, probably too fast.

"He left his clipboard here and I thought I could just fax his paperwork over to him if I knew his name. Not much I can do about the clipboard but I figured he needed his paperwork."

I was really going out on a limb because I didn't know if he carried a clipboard or not. Then Bud started to sound agitated.

"My brother is such an idiot. He probably has everything on there and doesn't even know where his next stop is. This is just like him, he never knows where he's going."

It registers with me that he said next stop, so he must not be going straight back to Atlanta. I've got to find out where he is going.

"Oh, I didn't mean to get him in trouble. It could be partially my fault. We got to talking about his rig and he set the clipboard down and then I moved it. I guess I distracted him and then he was in a hurry to get going. It was just an innocent mistake, nobody's fault really. Say, you know what? If you just want to give me his cell number I'll give him a call and make sure he has his next address and then I'll just fax this up to his next stop."

I'm really winging it now, hoping this fast talking will get me through.

"So, what is your brother's name again?"

"Greg, my dumb brother's name is Greg."

Then he softened a little, understanding that I am trying to help and he will be relieved of any of the work involved.

"Yeah that would work I guess, just make sure he has the Phoenix address of the import place on Thunderbird Road."

I fake searching for the paper, "hmm, let's see here, Thunderbird Road."

"Yes, it's an import stop"

"Yes, yes I see it here. I'll call right away."

"OK, here's his cell number. Are you ready?"

"Yes, go ahead."

"It's area code 404-361-5473"

He explained he's on the road today too, so that would

really be a help and actually thanked me.

Susan was standing right there by the table and she just slid into the empty chair. We did a high five in the air, both feeling a sense of relief, but for me it was short-lived. I had information that might help, but I didn't actually feel any closer to getting Diane back.

Next came the tricky part - should I call Killer who is now Greg? What should I say? I had bluffed my way so far, but I needed to do it one more time. Susan started to talk and I shushed her. I needed to concentrate. I snapped at her and I knew she was one more person I owed an apology, but right now I was focused on one thing. I had a plan and I had to jump right in before I lost my nerve. Would Killer answer his phone while driving a big rig? Well, he plays Scrabble while he drives, doesn't he?

LUNCH WITH DIANE AND GREG

Clipping along the highway, everything was unfamiliar but very much the same; lots of open spaces and miles of desert. Everything looked dry and uninviting. I started thinking terribly dark thoughts again. He could just pull this big truck over any time and end this ride for me. No one will ever find me. Is anyone looking yet? I don't even know, if I were them, where would I start? My thoughts are interrupted when Killer asks if I'm hungry.

"There's a place down here where we can eat. I don't get this way too often, but I remember it is good."

Every bad thought went out the window and we are friends now. He's not only talking food, he's talking good food and I was starving. My mind clicks back to Bob, my coat, food and finding a way to break away, all at the same time. I was almost happy for just a minute.

Things got quiet again and the miles seemed longer and I started seeing ads on billboards for a place called Peggy Sue's Diner. The prospect of going in somewhere to eat sounded too good to be true. I look like a homeless mess and this could be to my advantage. Maybe the way I look will draw some attention to me and someone will be looking. After our last stop, the gun was put back carefully on the floor board and it still made me nervous every time the truck went over a bump or rough spot. I found myself staring at it and turning away when Killer would turn my way and notice me looking at it. I needed to ignore it because I think it gave him a real power trip to keep me on edge this way. About five miles later, Killer downshifted, slowed down and pulled the big rig into Peggy Sue's.

Partly because of the size of the rig and partly, I'm sure because of me, Killer pulled way over to the furthest corner of the diner's parking Lot. I got a good look at the diner and it was the kind of place I would probably look for if I was out on a road trip with Brad. It's about time Killer did something nice for his new girlfriend, huh?

I still hadn't figured out the time, but I did notice that there were not a lot of cars in the lot and I surmised that it was later than lunch, but still not dinner time. I must have been delirious or something, but the prospect of getting out of this hunk of tin and into that diner really got me excited. Killer picks up his gun and slips it in his waist band and puts his light jacket back on. He swung his body out of the cab and then started to walk toward the back of the truck, instead of the front like he usually does. I twisted around to look, but I was unable to see past a certain point. I heard what sounded like a metal door opening, possibly a roll up type door on the rear of the truck. He opened my door which is conveniently out of sight of the front of the diner and reached in to clip my ankle tape. The freedom made me want to stomp my feet and shake them out, but I refrained, after all I was finally going to get out. Then to my dismay, he pulled me out and hustled me around to the rear of the truck. He picked me up in one swoop and deposited me in the trailer, fairly throwing me in. I hit hard and rolled on the hard metal floor. Killer started to bring the rolling door down.

"Hey, what are you doing?" I yelled.

In response, he jumped up into the back with me and grabbed me and pinned me down. Out came the tape and then I just couldn't help it, I started begging.

"No, please you said we could eat. I couldn't get out of here if I tried, you don't need to tape me. Just let me go in the diner, you can trust me."

I felt like I came off a little whiney and he appeared to be enjoying himself, and this really scared me. I was fighting now to no avail because this guy is strong and he slapped the first piece of tape on my mouth so I couldn't be heard and then wrapped my ankles and wrists together, forcing me into an uncomfortable ball. The floor was cold and hard and now for the first time since the threat at the rest stop, I was terrified. With his tape job finished, he got real close to my ear and talked in a low hissing voice that I hadn't heard before.

"Now see, you don't cooperate and you don't get to be comfortable anymore. You'll get to eat - you just got to settle down."

With that, he jumped out and I heard the metal door slam shut, and then I heard what sounded like a bolt and lock. I was safely locked away. Then it was just deadly silent, I couldn't even hear his footsteps as he walked away. I squirmed a bit and tried to situate myself with my back up against the wall of the truck, but I barely managed to do it.

It was so dark that it took a few minutes for my eyes to adjust and take in my surroundings. When I was finally able to see, I saw nothing but a big empty space to haul lots of stuff. I was happy that there wasn't a leftover casket from his last stop with my name on it. Again, I reminded myself that this is such a silly thought, guys like this wouldn't be using a casket. As I moved my head to scan my surroundings, the tape over my mouth was pulled over, far enough to be stuck in my hair and was pulling my hair, which really hurt. This was just one more thing to add to my already low point of this adventure, and I finally gave way to a good cry.

I thought about moving and trying to bang the side of the trailer, but I couldn't get in the right position and since I couldn't hear anyone, I figured they couldn't hear me. The idea of making noise seemed to be a waste of my energy and I had very little to waste. So, I cried and felt sorry for myself because I deserved a minute or two of pity. Besides, when he comes back, if he has any heart at all, maybe he will feel sorry for treating me so badly.

I knew he had a schedule to keep, so he probably would not be lingering over dinner, but it felt like hours. I had nothing to do but think, and that was probably not the best thing for me to do. For the first time, I reflected back to this morning, which seems like days ago, how stupid it was for me to leave that door open. If it had been locked, would he have abducted me later, maybe as I walked to the pharmacy? Speaking of the pharmacy, every time I coughed, I nearly choked myself with the tape covering my mouth. I bet Jack at the pharmacy wonders why I didn't come in. Did he understand the message I left and did Brad get the message from Jack? I could only pray someone out there was looking for me. My mind was starting to spin so fast, my head started to hurt. I totally avoided even thinking about Brad; I just couldn't bare it.

Finally, I heard the sound of the lock and bolt on the door as the huge metal door creaked open. As it opened, light came streaming in and I had to close my eyes, it was so blinding. Before I even opened my eyes, Killer was in and yanking me towards the door. In his rush to get me out, he dragged my body across the uneven floor and I felt grateful for the old gray sweats. He hastily removed all the duct tape, just in case we ran into anyone, but was careful to leave the tape on my mouth till the last minute. So much for trusting me. When he did rip it off, I cried out in pain and he slapped his hand over my mouth again. This time it felt like he took skin with it and the burning was terrible.

All the hairs caught up in the tape got pulled out too. He jumped down and lifted me down and rushed me back to my side of the truck. I tried to look around, hoping to see someone, but the place was dead quiet. Like one of his Scrabble plays, he would skip a turn to use all his tiles on his next play. I saw no one, which means no one saw me.

"You're making me late, we have to get out of here," was his only comment to me.

The door was slammed and he then quickly rushed to his side and started up the engine in one smooth move. As he turned the rig around and passed by the rear of the diner a kitchen door opened, and a guy with a white apron came out for a smoke. He glanced up at me and probably thought - this trucker must be traveling with his girlfriend. I somehow felt relieved that at least someone saw me, even if it didn't help at all.

It wasn't until we were on the main highway that he glanced over and shoved a small styrofoam container on the seat over to me. My hands and feet remained un-taped this time. Was he trusting me, in a hurry, or just getting sloppy? I wasn't going to ask, I just grabbed the container,

139

opened it and sank my teeth into the best cold, greasy grilled cheese sandwich I've ever had. It would have been nice to have something to wash it down with, but again, there are wants and there are needs. For this one moment, I am O.K. I couldn't help but think about sweet Chloe and her grilled cheese and fries on the boardwalk. That was such a nice day.

Every single billboard and sign by the side of the road told me we were indeed on our way to Phoenix. His scheduled pickup stop was going to be the next best opportunity to get away. He was going to be loading and he couldn't let anyone see me taped up, so what did he intend to do with me? What would I do with me? I tried to think of scenarios that might happen and I was pretty sure because of his silence he was doing the same thing. It was probably not so good for him to have all this thinking time, so I went back to trying some more small talk. I start with "thanks for the sandwich" and move on to "what are we going to pick up in Phoenix?" I got nothing but grunts and shrugs for answers; Killer didn't want to talk. Back to thinking. When we stop, maybe, I thought, I could scratch a message in the Styrofoam container and drop it where someone can find it. Maybe it's getting late enough that I could ask for my coat and get my hands on Bob. I had two other chances to make an escape and had failed both times. The fear of that gun is gripping and paralyzing me. Somehow, I needed to make an opportunity for myself and go for that bold move. The energy produced from a lukewarm grilled cheese sandwich was kicking in, I could feel it. I was suddenly jogged from my thoughts by a ring tone from my captor's cell phone. It had been hours and Killer's phone hadn't rung once. He looked a little startled to hear it. He grabbed his phone from his front shirt pocket and answered.

BRAD

The information that D and her captor were headed to an import depot on Thunderbird Road just wasn't enough. I needed a name and I needed an address. I had to pass on as much information to the police as possible - so it sounded believable and they took me seriously. At this hour of the day, Diane still was not an official missing person in their eyes. But if I had names and places and accurate information, they surely will follow up on it – right?

I tried googling Import places in Phoenix and even "Thunderbird Road" but to no avail. Nothing came up and I really needed to know what it was that was imported. I was nervous about cold calling Greg again, so I reviewed every option I could think of. I looked at the clock and it was already late afternoon. According to my calculations a person could drive direct to Phoenix in five and a half hours. If you add on maybe an hour for stops, food, gas, a restroom stop, you're still talking about maybe six and a half hours. A large 18 wheeler might take longer but even at that they should arrive at their destination any time now. The possibility that if I'm not able to get them stopped and they continue on to Atlanta terrified me. Not only were there several different routes that truckers take between those two cities, the trip is a twenty-six hour drive of over one thousand miles. The import stop, depending on what he had to pick up and how much of it there was, could buy us some extra time. If he had a huge load of stuff to get and not a lot of help loading it that could take some time. It could be furniture, or it could be Indian Jewelry for all I knew. It sure would have been nice to know.

All this information and lack of information had me up and pacing the floor. Susan wasn't helping; every time I look at her she had a pleading panicked look on her face.

"I really need to call Greg again and bluff some information out of him, Susan. What do you think?"

Her worries were the same as mine. What if I goof up and tip him off and he takes it out on Di? I reasoned that he needs to get to Phoenix and do his job and this could be a safety net for us. Susan was quick to point out that if he got spooked and thinks someone is on to him, maybe he would skip Phoenix and just keep going to who knows where. Susan tends to be negative, so I tried to ignore her idea, but I have to admit it had already occurred to me as well.

"Susan, did you get that bag together for me to take to Di? How about you go out and put it in my car?"

I tossed her my keys from across the room, she made an

amazing catch and she was out the door. I really needed her gone if only for a few minutes. As soon as she was out of the apartment, I took one deep breath and called the cell phone number for Greg 'Killer' Adams.

The phone rang once, twice, three times and then I heard a deep male voice.

"Adams Brothers Trucking, Greg Adams speaking, what can I do for you?"

My blood ran cold, I was talking to this creep and he had D with him, I just knew it. I couldn't stop now - I have to jump right in with one of my best stories yet.

"Hey, yeah, this is Phoenix here and I'm wondering if you could give me your E.T.A. My main warehouse guy had to take off early 'cause his wife went into labor and I've got to stay here till you get this shipment picked up."

I was talking fast and giving him too much information, hoping he doesn't notice I just called the whole business 'Phoenix' for lack of a name. Greg Adams didn't seem to notice and answered,

"Well, let's see it's about four and I'm probably about an

hour out – does that help?"

I was quick to notice he says I and not we. Does that mean anything? He almost sounded nice and that really had me bugged.

"Hey Buddy, that really helps, thanks so much. Oh, one more thing before I let you go, which address did they give you? We have the office down the road here from the warehouse and it's always a confusion. Sometimes, the drivers get the wrong address and it's such a bother to them when they end up at the office."

I hear some paper shuffle and can tell he's buying this. He snapped at the bait, so to speak, and gave it to me.

"let's see, it looks like 1241 E. Thunderbird – that sound right?"

I keep this charade going,

"that's great, perfect, the gal at the front desk will be looking for you and direct you around back to the loading area. Her name is Lola."

I hope like crazy he will do what I want him to do. Again,

he grabs the bait and repeats the name just as I thought he might.

"OK, Lola, I can't forget that one, she sounds like a hot number."

He finished with a big belly laugh - that was the Greg that I had expected to hear.

"Yes, she is really something, you'll see!"

I laugh with him like we are two dirty ol' men sharing a real good joke. Somehow, I just wanted to keep talking, knowing that Di was probably sitting just a foot or two away from him. For this one moment, I felt close to her. I got this mental picture of her and wished in some way I could comfort her. Will she catch the reference to Lola? I can only hope she picked up on it. I know I can't keep this conversation going. I say good-bye and hang up. It was a terrible feeling saying goodbye to Greg and feeling I'm saying good-bye to Diane.

Susan came back in quietly at the end of our conversation and heard the last few words. She is grinning this time and said she didn't realize what a great liar I was, but she would definitely forgive me, just this once. We were looking at each other and I know we were contemplating the same question, what's next?

I got out my wallet, fished out my credit card and flipped it to Susan at the same moment she tossed my keys to Lola back to me. We did it with such precision that I would have to admit we were making a good team after all. I explained I needed a round trip ticket for myself and a one way back for D right away, the first flight out. There was no time to do a lot of talking, the clock was ticking. If Killer got to Thunderbird Road and ran into all my lies before someone arrested him, then he would know he had been caught up with. The thought that he might take it out on Di is something that was on my mind continually. There might not be a front desk at this import place and there surely wasn't a Lola. I had the address jotted on a scrap of paper in my front pocket and I jogged down the walk to my car. I opened the door, jumped in, and started her up. Pulling onto the street to drive to the police station, I wished this wasn't happening. I wished I could just drive and drive all the way to Arizona and fix everything.

147

This seemed like something I needed to do face to face. The station was probably five minutes away and if I called, I might wait fifteen minutes for an officer. My last experience told me they couldn't do much more than write out a report. Traffic was with me and I pulled into the parking lot and sprinted to the building in record time. As soon as I got in, I started talking to everyone and anyone who would listen and right away, they ushered me into a small cubicle with a desk. The Lieutenant was polite and attentive. I pulled out the cards the officers had given me earlier in the day and tried to relate the whole story as quickly as I could, not leaving anything out. I told him about the Scrabble game and the 'Words With Friends' part. He seemed interested, but I worked hard, trying to get him to see the urgency of my story. I pleaded with him.

"We have less than an hour to meet him at the address I have on Thunderbird Road. This is an estimate and could be off one way or the other, but at any rate this is cutting it really close."

He explained to me that if this is true that this man, Greg

148

Adams, has taken Diane Masters across state lines then he has to forward all of this to the proper Arizona agency. All I could think of is how long will this take? I know he's trying to help, but I had a strong urge to jump across the table and grab the guy - police officer or not. I refrained. He began a lot of typing and phoning while I tried my hardest to remain quiet and calm. After a couple of minutes, he pushed some paperwork my way and exited the cubicle. I felt fairly certain that he believed this whole crazy story but who really knows what they think when someone gives them a story like this.

He returned within minutes and told me I can leave, but to keep my cell phone on and he would try to keep me informed. I was out of the door with those words and I decided I wouldn't tell him I was on my way to Phoenix.

Dashing to the parking lot, I got Susan on the line. She started her conversation with, "You're booked." Then gave me the details; the flight was on Jet Blue out of Long Beach and leaves at 8:15 arriving at 9:30. My heart sank at the times she gave, then perked up when she explained - There's another flight leaving right away, she didn't book it because she really didn't think I could make it there in time. It's possible that they had room on the flight and might be able to switch the tickets but the timing was crucial. Nothing at this point was impossible.

I jumped into the car and sped to the airport. Because of business trips and travel to visit my parents, I knew that if the traffic was light I could be there in twenty minutes. Talk about a chance to try Lola out, this was it. I was on the freeway in minutes and driving like every other aggressive obnoxious California driver on the road. I'm usually the conservative driver, but under the circumstances I was doing all the Nascar moves, pedal to the metal, darting in and out of traffic. It really went against my grain but I had no choice. In my rush, I forgot to ask Susan what time the flight left and I'm glad I didn't. At this point it was better for me not to know. I wasn't looking at the time on the dash, I was just driving - fast. I didn't have room in my brain to calculate leaving time, travel time, arrival time – I just had to take this one step at a time – step one, get to the airport. I pushed redial on my cell phone and put it on speaker.

"Susan, could you do a quick check for me on a rental car? I'll text you from the airport and let you know if I get out on the earlier flight."

The next twenty minutes was a blur. Once at the airport, I parked, grab D's overnight bag and ran. At the ticket desk, they informed me that the plane is loading and since I don't have any check in, I can board. I impatiently told her this is like a real emergency and she rushed the paper work and called ahead to the gate that the last passenger was on his way. I texted Susan a quick "YES!" Thanking the ticket agent while in a full run, I slipped off my shoes and belt and emptied my pockets as I rushed towards the security check. I'm positive this has never been done faster – I was holding my shoes in my hand as I boarded the plane. I got the usual welcome, along with a little giggle from the flight attendants. I must have really looked a mess. I ran my hand through my hair and stood there with a girlie-looking pink overnight bag, not even knowing my seat number. A flight attendant was kind enough to escort me to it as I tried to ignore annoyed looks along the way. She gave me a sympathetic pat on the shoulder and I buckled up, clutching Diane's bag snugly in my lap. The attendant offered to put it in the overhead luggage compartment, but I just shook my head no. All I knew at this moment was that this is all I have of her and I felt like I could break down at any minute – I have to keep it together I kept telling myself.

This was going to be the longest short flight ever. I felt a strange feeling in the pit of my stomach, only to realize I hadn't had a thing to eat all day and this flight is too short to be serving pretzels and drinks. I felt selfish for this moment of thought, not knowing what D has been going through. I couldn't let my imagination dwell on this though, it would have made me physically sick.

This thinking brings me to the realization that I don't want to live without Diane. I am madly, unequivocally in love with this girl and it just can't end this way. As the plane lifts off the runway and my body was being pushed back against the seat, the feeling reminded me that I was not in control of anything at this point.

About six months ago, I almost proposed to D, but the night before I planned to propose, we got into this deep conversation. That night, she told me how great it was that she never felt pressured by me and never felt like she was being rushed into doing something she wasn't ready to do. It was a real deal breaker. I decided she needed more time and I was OK with that at the time. Now, I was feeling entirely different about the subject. I concluded that I should have been more assertive and talked her into it, as I knew I probably could have. If I had proposed six months ago, we might already be married and maybe everything would be different today. When I find her, things are going to be different, I need a commitment. But for now, I told myself, I must turn my brain off and stop thinking about this. I stared out the window at the clouds and this gave me a sense of calm that I hadn't felt for hours. For the rest of the flight, I must think about nothing but clouds.

In situations like this, time usually drags but instead, the hour and fifteen minutes flew by quickly and it seems like we were barely off the ground and it was time to descend. My mind turned back on because I knew I needed to get off this plane faster than anyone else and on my way. Positive thinking now - I'm ready to see D. I needed to hit the ground running, yet I didn't know for sure where I was heading.

I should have a text waiting for me that tells me which car rental agency is holding a car for me, thanks to Susan. It's exactly six forty-five and if everything went well Di could be waiting safely for me somewhere.

Just like my crazy drive to the airport, I become this pushy pedestrian that didn't care what other people thought. I snake my way through the line of people, holding my pink bag high over my head. Of course, I say "excuse me" but we all know that type of person really doesn't mean it – I was that person.

The airport is a small one and I quickly and rudely navigated my way to the car rental area. Susan had called ahead just as we planned, and a nice little compact car was waiting for me. It certainly wasn't Lola, but it would get the job done. I quickly asked for some directions, threw D's bag in the passenger seat and I was on my way.

ONE HOUR TO PHOENIX

At the sound of the ringtone, Killer pulled his cellphone from his front shirt pocket. It had been a long day driving and this is the first call. I was startled by the ring since I never noticed that he had a phone on him and he seemed a bit startled himself.

"Adams Brothers Trucking, Greg Adams speaking. What can I do for you?"

Really, couldn't he just have told me his name is Greg when I asked him? He reached for a clipboard, hung on a hook on his dash. He was driving and talking and flipping the pages to confirm information with the caller. He gave an estimated time of arrival at his next stop at five o'clock and confirms with the caller an address. The conversation seemed pretty normal. He was overly nice and polite to this person who was probably his customer and then he sounded like he was joking around with him. Then what he said really grabbed my attention. Killer said he will remember some girl's name and the name is Lola. He was going on about how she must be a hot number and he's laughing that kind of wicked laugh guys do when they talk about girls that way. My heart started to pound so hard I was afraid he would hear it. I looked straight ahead, hoping he didn't notice the startled expression on my face. Was this a coincidence or could this be Brad on the phone trying to fish for information? It sounded so much like something he might do. Maybe I was so desperate that I was reading too much into the name. Killer hung up and continued to chuckle to himself.

I was thinking about Bob again and wished I could have him just to call Brad and let him know I got the clue. It's still hot out and I have no reason to ask for the coat. The question again came to me: how does he think he is going to load up this truck and keep me in place and quiet. My hands and feet remain unbound since our little dinner break, he can't throw me in the back of the truck. I was wondering if this is worrying him too, or did he have a plan. I decided the more talking I do, the less time he will have to figure this out, so it's back to talking.

"Hmm, Greg huh? That's a nice name. Greg sounds a lot nicer than Killer. I had a good friend growing up named Greg."

I was rambling and for some reason, I had a surge of confidence that I was winning the game. He still wasn't answering me, but he did that thing, where he shifts his weight like he is uncomfortable. I decided I could keep this up and irritate him for the next hour.

"So, it's OK if I just call you Greg, huh?"

Still no answer, so I continue to use his name over and over.

"Greg, we sure are getting to Phoenix fast, I never knew Phoenix was this short of a drive."

I was even irritating myself at this point.

"Greg, I never knew that these big rigs gave you such a smooth ride, is there a lot of maintenance on one of these things?"

I thought I detected just the smallest drop of perspiration dripping down Greg's brow and sure enough, he reached up and gave it a wipe.

"Greg, I'm sorry, but you know what, I don't think I even thanked you for that sandwich, what am I thinking?"

At this point, he had reached his boiling - point, I had pushed it as far as I could. His big hand made a fist and he slammed it down on the seat right between us.

"I'm trying to drive here, so just shut-up!"

"Nice play," I said to myself.

As I gazed out the window, I saw several restaurant and motel signs by the side of the freeway. I noticed that most of them were close by - a mile or two away. He must have got his timing off because if my observations were correct we should have been approaching Phoenix. It wasn't more than ten minutes before this that he told his caller an hour. Not more than five miles pass as I was thinking this and Killer downshifted and slowed, then exited at the offramp. As we pulled off the road, I saw only one thing; something that made my heart sink - a large neon sign in front of an old motel called the Desert Sun Motor Lodge. Could this be the last place I would ever see?

As the truck came to a complete stop on the gravel driveway, I decided then and there that this wasn't going to happen! With both arms, I reached for the handle of the door and push down with every ounce of energy I have. Killer lunges for me and grabs me by the arm and yanks me back into the cab. He is faster and bigger and I knew I didn't have a chance, but I had to try. He threw himself on me as he grabbed an old rag and stuffed it into my mouth. Still holding on, he reached down for the gun and shoved it my side. Then he was on his phone.

"Hey Junie, it's me Greg, I'm right out front. Did you leave number ten open for me? I don't have time to check in because I need to finish loading up at my stop here in Phoenix, but I'm going to do a quick change and throw my stuff in the room. I'll be back in about an hour, hour and a half. I'll settle up with you then, OK? I gotta' get this rig loaded up."

Killer shoved the pistol harder against my ribs, reminding me who was in control.

"Thanks sweetie, see you when I get back. I know I can always count on you."

Greg was one step ahead of me again, he had this all planned out for another killer play. He's done this before.

159

He knew exactly where to park around back and close to the last unit, which is apparently number ten, his special room. He turned the engine off, dashed around the front of the truck in full sight with his gun in the air, so I am sure to see it. I was frozen with fear and felt paralyzed so much so that when he opened the door to yank me out, my legs had turned to jelly. This made him angrier because he wanted me to walk with him to his 'special room.'

"Fine," I said to myself, "if this is the way you're going to be then it's just going to be harder."

So, going around the corner with him half dragging me with the gun pressed hard in my side, he gave door number ten a kick and the door swung open as he shoved me in.

A quick look around told me this was not the honeymoon suite. The room was dingy, vintage seventies, dark with a stale tobacco smell. He shoved me on the bed and closed the safety bolt on the door. This time, there was no talk. I was fighting for everything I was worth, but he pinned me down quickly.

"Now, if I could just trust you for a minute, I could take

this rag out of your mouth."

He seemed to have barely worked up a sweat, but I was dripping and shaking as I nodded my head in agreement, so I could get this rag out of my mouth. He pulled it out as I coughed and sputtered and spit. He started to speak in a smooth steady tone, still pinning me and holding the gun to my side.

"Listen, I don't have time for this!"

His voice was almost pleading.

"I need to trust you, and you keep making it hard for me to do that. I have a job to do and I'm going to leave you here and you can't go all crazy on me. So, you have to understand you're just going to be a little uncomfortable for a while."

This was the softest I'd ever heard him speak and it got my attention for that reason only. Now, he took his time and taped and tied me up carefully. No sloppy job this time, I was not going anywhere. I gave up the struggle and let him do it - grateful that tying me up is the only thing he is doing to me. For now at least.

My only hope is that he would leave soon and buy me some time to figure my way out of this mess. If there was a flaw in his tie-up job, I didn't want him to know it then, I wanted to find out after he left. Laying very still, he carefully covered my eyes tightly and everything went dark.

Although not being able to see, I could hear everything clearly. I heard the floor squeak when he moved about the room and I heard him walk out of the room, but only for a minute. I heard the door of the truck slam shut and I heard him walking back towards the room. Then the door safety latch closes again. He headed to the bathroom and I could hear the shower running.

In my mind I pictured the water running down over me, washing all the dirt and sweat and grime away. When the water stopped, I heard the rustling of clothes as he changed. I felt the heat of the room and the heat of my body from the wrestling, and I felt the prickly wetness of perspiration dripping down my face with no way to wipe it off. I also had the feeling in the quietness of the room that he was only inches away from me. Suddenly, my whole body jerked when I felt him place a cold washcloth against my face. Is this, I asked myself, where the captive is supposed to fall for her captor? Fat chance. It wasn't going to happen, not in a million years. He said nothing, which really added to the creepiness of the situation.

"Please just leave," I thought to myself.

I heard the door shut and I remained frozen - still and quiet, until finally, I heard the metal door slam and the engine start. Thank God, he was really leaving.

There seemed to be no flaw in his bondage skills. I tried to rock my body, to bang the bed against the wall but I remember that the bed is on the far wall and not on the wall that adjoins to the unit next door. Killer had thought of everything.

His time line was an hour and a half and as I figured it, the half was already gone.

BRAD

I followed the directions to the stationhouse that was supposedly in charge of Diane's case. Everyone was nice enough, but no one seemed to know about any arrest of a Greg Adams. I'd been snooping around for about a half hour and I didn't see or hear any indication that Diane was here anywhere waiting for me. A detective who looked like he would know what's going on, kept going in and out of different offices carrying papers and looking important, so I finally got the nerve to ask him if he could help me. - Did he know anything about an arrest of a truck driver on Thunderbird Road? He was very sympathetic and said no but said he would go and see what he could find out for me. He told me to relax and have a seat and offered me coffee. In a few minutes he returned with a couple of donuts that might have been real tasty about eight hours previously, but I scarfed them down like they were truly the best things I had ever wrapped my mouth around. He leaves to get me some information and I resort to grabbing a nearby pencil and drumming it nervously on the bench I'm sitting on. Sugar in a high dose from the donuts probably wasn't the best thing for me, but at least I didn't have to worry about finding myself something to eat.

I looked up at the clock. Time was really getting away

from me. If they haven't apprehended Greg Adams by now, he is on the road to Atlanta. He can't possibly drive all day and all night, so he would have to stop somewhere along the way. Maybe his brother would have that information if I called him. Surely, if I spelled this all out he would co-operate with me, right? After all he was telling me what an idiot his brother was when I talked to him earlier. As I was running these thoughts through my head, the detective returned and sat down next to me on the bench. He had some official looking papers in his hands and he was doing a lot of flipping them back and forth.

"O.K. what we have here, is information that Mister Adams was stopped at Kim's Imports on Thunderbird Road at six fifteen this evening. He was questioned and found to be carrying and un-licensed firearm on his person at that location."

"And?"

I could feel myself sucking in air in anticipation of the next sentence.

"And he has been brought in for further questioning and

according to everything I can see here, due to information from an informant outside of the state, he is being held for suspicion of kidnapping, but at this time is not under arrest. He was not found to have anyone traveling with him."

I really needed to have that statement repeated because it didn't compute. It's impossible - my girlfriend should be in that truck! I suddenly lost control.

"No, no you don't understand, he took my girlfriend. He took Diane from her apartment in California. She's IN HIS TRUCK!"

Now I was screaming and waving my arms as the detective was attempting to calm me.

"Now just wait - let's just calm down. I'm sure we will get to the bottom of this. The truth is out there and this is our job to find out what's going on."

This wasn't helping. I wanted to tear this place up and find this creep myself. I'll personally beat the truth out of him. The detective kept his cool while I was flailing.

"It's going to be OK really, my guys here are very thorough - We'll find her."

Slowly, I regained some of my composure.

"Come on now, let's go down the hall here and see if we can make you comfortable while we sort this out."

He ushered me to a small room where a pleasant lady sat at her desk.

"Madge, this is Brad and he's here trying to find his missing girlfriend. Could you call over to one of the hotels across the way and see if you can get him a room and anything else he needs. I don't know how long this is going to take and he can't stay here in the hallway all day."

Then he turned to me.

"You go get a little rest and clean up, you've had a hard day. I promise that I will personally call you the minute we find out anything."

I was feeling like a big dumb kid at the principal's office and I didn't like the idea of being shuffled off, but what could I possibly do but wait?

While waiting for Madge to make calls, I got out the phone and scrolled through a dozen texts; one from my boss and the rest from Susan. I wish I had something positive to tell them and I didn't want to send them a negative message, so I just skipped it. I couldn't do it. This wasn't looking good at all.

THE HOLIDAY INN, PHOENIX ARIZONA

I stuck the keycard in the slot on the door and entered my room. Tossing the pink bag on the spare bed and wondering what I need with one bed, let alone two queen size beds, I stepped over to the window and pulled the heavy drapes open. It was somewhat of a comfort that my only view was the huge three story building that I just left – the Phoenix Police station, court house and correctional facility. If I got into one of those beds and fell asleep, I might miss something, so I just sat in a desk chair and stared at the buildings. I hadn't checked the time in a while and I wondered to myself if it even mattered at this point. I noticed the sky slowly turning a warm, orange hue around the buildings. This has been the longest day of my life and the craziest thing is that Diane Masters is still not officially missing because it had not yet been twenty-four hours.

I tried to digest what I had been told. A sickening feeling hit me when I recalled that Greg Adams was carrying a gun. I vowed in my head not to call him Killer anymore. I mentally kicked myself that I didn't ask all the questions I wanted to ask. The shock of the moment had paralyzed me. I reached into my pocket and pulled out the calling card that detective James Sykes had given me and I had a passing thought to call him, but then I decided to give it some time and let him do his job. I started thinking crazy stuff like getting in the rental car and driving to Thunderbird Road, but how crazy would that be? Diane is simply not there.

Getting up only for a minute, I was drawn to D's pink travel bag on the bed. I picked it up, unzipped it and proceeded to drop its entire contents on the bed and then picked up each item and carefully examine it. I had no idea if I was looking for something or why I'm doing this. What if this is all I have of her? What if I never see her again? Partly out of fear and partly out of anger, I threw every item back in the bag.

It was time to make a few calls, so I reluctantly grabbed my phone and got to it. I thought about texting, but it seemed so cold and besides that, I felt like I needed to hear a familiar voice or two. I started with Susan because I knew she was worried sick and deserved to have some of her questions answered. She answered on the first ring and she was nearly in a hysterical state. I wished with every fiber of my being that I had good news to tell her to make her feel better. At least Diane's abductor has been apprehended, but the harsh reality is that she is still missing. After a couple minutes of weak assurances, I told Susan I had to get off the line in case a call came through. That of course was true, but the bigger truth was I just couldn't talk about it anymore. I composed myself, took a deep breath and called my boss. For some reason, it was easier to tell him every detail, probably because I knew he wasn't going to break down on me. He listened and sympathized and was reassuring with every word. After all, just because Greg had a gun doesn't mean he had used it. By the way, they will be checking the weapon and will determine if he has fired it recently. Like I said, reasonable and comforting with every word.

170

While I was at it, I decided it was only fair to call my parents. It's not that I wanted to worry them, but somehow, I felt if I shared the worry, it would relieve me of some of it, as crazy as that sounds. Mom was ready to jump on a plane, but I convinced her to hold tight, I would keep them posted. I convinced her that I was doing OK. Another lie.

Back at the chair by the window, I decided to keep my vigil and stare at that building across the way. The sun had officially set now and soon it would be too dark to see anything, but I still felt that I needed to stand watch. I considered taking a shower, I considered room service, I even considered that big bed. But I did nothing.

There comes a time, however, when you convince yourself that it wouldn't hurt to just rest your eyes for a couple of minutes and that's what I did. As I drifted off I reminded myself that I am a very light sleeper and if I do fall asleep, the slightest thing will wake me. The slightest thing was light streaming in the window at daybreak.

I jumped out of my chair and grabbed the phone I found lying on the floor, as it had apparently been on my lap all night long. First, I checked the time - six A.M! I checked to see if there are any texts or calls I might have missed. Nothing. I gave myself a brush off and noticed that I have an unbelievable case of wrinkles going on. There's a big bar of soap and a brush in that bag, but I didn't have the forethought to pack myself a change of clothes. I never in a million years thought I'd be where I am, needing a change of clothes.

I guess it was a Boy Scout mentality that kicked in next. I retrieved the charger out of D's stuff and plugged my phone in the bathroom, so I would not miss anything. Then I hung my clothes on hangers in the bathroom and turned the shower on to get it steamy and jumped in for a quick shower. This wasn't going to be great, but at this point, anything would be an improvement. The result was I felt a little bit better and looked not a whole lot better. I grabbed my barely charged phone and headed down to the lobby. I must be realistic here. I needed to eat something so I could navigate this day with a clear mind.

The Holiday Inn breakfast bar wasn't bad but it wasn't good either – it was just food. I ate too fast, but it was what I needed to get going.

THE DESERT SUN MOTOR LODGE

Hopefully, sooner or later I will hear someone and if I do, I'll try to make some kind of noise. I made one last effort to shake something loose. Killer had done a real good job this time, no doubt about it. With every strenuous effort, I felt an overwhelming exhaustion and I decided to simply lie still and listen carefully. I figured that in less than an hour Greg would return. I started counting to myself, so I didn't lose track of time. The effect was something like counting sheep and before I knew it, I was out cold. When I came to, I had no idea what time it was. Everything was dark and the sheer terror of the situation was intensified, not knowing when that door would open. I then started the longest wait of my life. Maybe there had been a change of plans. If that was really Brad on the phone, maybe Greg has been arrested. What if no one knows where to look for me? Or what if Greg has just given up, afraid of coming back to get me and just left me here. I reasoned to myself that this could be the best scenario because some time tomorrow afternoon, someone will no doubt come in and make up the room. I count in my head how many hours that might be and decide that this is still better than having Killer come back. I tried to block out every negative thought in my mind and I allowed my mind to dream about anything and everything good that has ever happened to me. Most of my thoughts turned to Brad since he is the best thing in my life. I remembered an evening about six months ago when we had such a nice long talk and I told him one of the things I loved about him the most. It was how I appreciated that he never pushed or pressured me. I wondered if we would be married now had I never said that. Then, perhaps I wouldn't be in this mess.

I was more uncomfortable than I'd ever been in my entire life, but I had to keep reminding myself that I am still alive, the game wasn't over yet.

JAMES SYKES, DONUTS AND A WALMART

I was so close, I decided to walk over to again try to find Detective Sykes, even though I hadn't received a call or text. Surely, he has some kind of update on what's going on. I asked for him and got forwarded to several different locations in the building. The guy seemed to be everywhere, and everyone seemed to know him. I really felt as if I was a bother to these people, but they must understand how important this was to me. I finally located Sykes by nearly being run over by him in the hallway. He greeted me like an old friend with a slap on the shoulder.

"Hey, my man, were you able to get some sleep? You look a little better than you did last night."

I was glad for his concern, but I didn't have time for all the small talk. Not to be rude, but rather than answer him, I blasted right into questions, some of which I should have asked earlier. James ushered me into one of the closest cubicles and motions for me to have a seat.

"Brad, I've been following this real close for you and you have to understand that these things take time. When I have something concrete, I will let you know right away. What we do know is this: Mister Adams has been questioned extensively and he is not telling us much. My guys are out at the Thunderbird Road location, where we picked him up, and have thoroughly gone through his truck. I know this isn't what you want to hear, but we must have something to hold him on. If we can find something, then we can book him."

I was starting to get the picture that they would need to find evidence of a crime - and if they didn't find that, this guy would walk. Could they connect D with him? Would they even try?

Then came the offer of coffee and donuts; I figured they would be fresher than the last time around, but I really was not in the mood.

"So, what now?" I asked.

"The guys will be in the field for a while yet. Remember I told you they are real thorough? Then when they come back they might have lab work, fingerprints, who knows."

I could tell now he was measuring his words with me. I knew without the words spoken, they are looking for blood samples or other evidence of a crime and I got that real sick feeling because this was Di we are talking about, not just a crime victim.

"Do you know if the guys' gun has been fired recently?"

176

Of course, the answer was that he couldn't say at this time. I started getting the feeling that there are a lot of things he couldn't say and maybe things he knows that he doesn't want me to know. Deep down, I understand, but my frustration level, from one to ten, was a twelve.

He made the suggestion that I relax and wait for further developments. Really? Is that what most guys would do when their girlfriend goes missing? Wouldn't it seem strange if I went over to the Hotel and took a soak in the Jacuzzi? I tried hard to put on my most polite face and told the detective I would check back around noon.

Crossing the road, I decided to take a ride in my rental car around town. I thought I might just swing by Thunderbird Road, you know, just to see the truck. I might run into a Walmart or somewhere where I could pick up some boxers and a shirt and some other things I need. Yeah, you know, just to "relax". These guys didn't know me.

I wasn't too interested in the Walmart shopping spree just yet, so I started driving to the address I had on Thunderbird Road. As it turned out, I didn't need the number. As soon as I got a block away, I saw a beehive of police cars and

177

activity. I also could see that great big white rig I had seen just a day earlier on the Coast Highway by Diane's apartment. With a huge lump in my throat, I just turned around and went the other way. They wouldn't appreciate me being there. Next stop, somewhere to make me presentable.

After picking up a few things, I drove slowly around the area, and tried to stretch the morning out - noon seemed so far away. Eventually I circled back to the hotel to drop off my clothing purchases. Checking the time, it was only ten fifteen and I was driving around aimlessly. I dropped a quick text to Susan, filling her in on what I knew. Nothing to tell her really, but that adage of "no news is good news" kept coming to mind. Surely these guys would know something by now.

The detective didn't say it, but I thought there must be a time limit to how long they could keep this guy locked up without charging him, so they would want to work as fast as they could.

I decided it's time to call my parents again. It sounded as if Mom picked up the phone in anticipation of it ringing. I can tell she had a bad night and it makes me feel guilty that I had slept. To my dismay, in the middle of our conversation, my phone makes a beeping noise and then goes dead. Great timing, I thought. I just put the phone on the charger and took a walk. I literally didn't know what to do with myself. I decided to walk around and eventually make my way over to the stationhouse. They weren't going to call me before noon anyway.

THE LONG NIGHT AT THE DESERT SUN.

It didn't take long for me to realize that something wasn't going as planned. Perhaps Killer has been arrested or maybe having me with him isn't as much fun as he thought it would be.

The motel was close enough to the main highway that I could hear the traffic. I detected a difference in the traffic patterns and assumed it must be night time. As hard as I tried, I heard zero activity around the motel. I tried to determine what day it was and reminded myself that if it was nighttime, it was still Monday - and Monday probably isn't a big travel day. The truth may be that the Desert Sun

Motor Lodge wasn't a 5 star travel destination.

The wind blew with a gust each time large trucks whizzed by and the old motel creaked. Every creak is terrifying and sent chills down my spine. My body was hot one minute and cold the next, and I start to wonder if I was getting sicker. My mind was faltering, and I felt completely disoriented. I decided that it was doing me no good to try to think things out. Simply put, my brain was hurting, my body was hurting, and I was exhausted. I stopped fighting and drifted off into another fitful sleep. I awoke and drifted off for what seems like forever. Each time I awoke, I was more unclear about where I was and what I was doing here.

Suddenly I awoke to voices outside the window and was trying to make sense of what was going on. I heard a female voice and a male voice and the jangling of keys. The female voice must be that of Junie the motel manager, because she was explaining that this was the room that Mr. Adams usually rents, and if his truck wasn't here then he wasn't here. My body went limp when I heard the turning of the key and the door swinging open. I had been so tense for so long that my body didn't know how to react to the relief of being saved.

I must have looked dead because I heard a collective gasp and footsteps and noise. Immediately, helpful hands were working to remove the tape form my eyes and mouth – to free me and talk to me and make me comfortable. Paramedics and police were rushing in and doing what they do and their kindness was overwhelming; I begin to sob and cry and cough; It's over, I'm alive, I can go home.

As I was transported through the door and towards a waiting ambulance, I took a quick look around the room and it appeared more awful than I remembered from my brief glance yesterday. I asked what time it was and what day it was and yes, it was finally Tuesday morning, 10:15 A.M.

They asked about my condition on the way to the hospital and I told them I was fine, I wanted to go home. They explained in a blur that I was dehydrated, and I needed to be checked out and the police needed to ask me some questions. I was hooked up to an I.V. on the way and although the paramedic apologized for hurting me, I didn't

181

feel a thing.

In the hospital I was besieged by examinations and questions for over two hours. Then, police investigators began with their debriefing. I decided I have some questions to ask them. "How did they find me at the motel? Did they arrest Greg Adams? Was it possible for them to get me my coat? Can I call my boyfriend because he was in California and was probably worried sick about me?

I learn from the detectives that they combed through the entire truck and retrieved Greg's cell phone. The last call made on it was to the Desert Sun Motor Lodge and so they went there and found me. Pretty simple really. They have Greg Adams in custody and he will be booked for numerous charges, including kidnapping and a firearm charge. They needed me to fill out a formal complaint, but said we could do that when they take me over to police headquarters. My coat was put in the evidence bag and I could have that as soon as they check out everything and take pictures for their records. And, oh yes, I can call that boyfriend of mine anytime I want. The officer offered me his phone. My hand was shaking as I took it and I wished I had Bob in my hand instead. I had to think hard about the number, after all, Bob always takes care of those details for me. I'm pretty sure I got it right, but to my dismay there was no answer. Darn - of all times for him not to answer. The officer continued,

"Oh and by the way Greg Adams phone showed one other call that he received about five o'clock. We traced it to a Brad Cummings, does that name mean anything to you? We need to check that guy out."

I grinned from ear to ear just hearing the name; I knew it. It WAS Brad who really found me!

A nurse came in to fill out release forms. She assured me the that the bruises and bumps are all minor and I should heal very quickly. The doctor has recommended that I take a few days off to get plenty of rest and to drink lots of liquids. She also suggested that I see my family doctor at home just to be sure about everything and especially if I have any concerns or problems.

"By the way, do you need us to give you a prescription for

that cough?"

That actually made me laugh – "No, it's OK, I think I have something at home".

The officers returned to let me know they had a patrol car out front and were ready to get me over to the station.

"We have someone there to help you make arrangements to get you home, and make sure you get your belongings out of evidence."

They put me in a wheel chair and wheeled me out. I am tired and sore, but I feel like I could run all the way home if they would let me.

Once we were in the station, they sat me in a small office at the end of a hallway. A nicely dressed female officer took all the information from me about my ordeal. For the first time, it dawned on me how horrible I must look. The logistics of me getting home sounded crazy to me. I certainly couldn't get on a plane looking like this. I answer all her questions to the best of my wobbling ability, but some things seemed harder to say than I thought they would be. She got me a cup of water because my throat was so dry and asked if I needed something to eat. Food, now there is something I hadn't thought of for quite a while. She got on the phone,

"Could you have something sent up from the cafeteria to my office?"

Turning towards me, with her hand covering the phone she relays a message from the cafeteria.

"How does a grilled cheese sandwich sound to you?"

"Wonderful, thank you." I smiled and rolled my eyes.

She continued to make out the report and glanced up at me mid-sentence,

"We need to get you cleaned up and figure out how to get you home, huh?"

"Yes, that would be good."

A second officer came in with a large bag and I jumped to my feet on seeing it.

"Bob, oh I need Bob."

I could tell by the look they gave me, they thought I was

delirious. He carefully sat the bag at my feet and backed out of the room, leaving officer number one to deal with the crazy girl. I rummaged through the bag, pulled out the coat and began to check the pockets. Bob had been removed and was floating around at the bottom of the bag - which put me into a panic for a few seconds. But soon I had my hand wrapped around my old friend.

"Meet Bob, he's my B.F.F," I said, smiling and holding him out proudly.

I didn't think how crazy that sounded until it came out of my mouth.

"Ah, and it looks like he took a tumble and got a crack on his face," said the female officer.

Her tone was very sympathetic. I thought about telling her he'd been that way for a while, but I just muttered under my breath that "he must have gotten dropped in the truck." – The lie continues.

Another female officer popped her head in with a plastic cafeteria tray in hand.

"Phoenix's finest grilled cheese delivery service here," she announced with a smile.

It was accompanied by a soda with ice and a straw, and tasted heavenly. Just to draw something cold and sugary up into my parched mouth was the best feeling ever. Then I opened the Styrofoam container and there it was, the most awesome grilled cheese sandwich I have ever laid my eyes on. I couldn't help it, I started laughing hysterically. As the officer looked up over her glasses she asked, "Is everything OK?"

"Yep, everything is just fine and you are going to witness me eating the last grilled cheese I'll ever eat."

That remark got a quizzical look and a shrug and then she was back to her typing.

HIGH NOON IN PHOENIX

I always have prided myself on being in good physical shape, but I guess the weird eating and sleeping and worry has caught up with me. I have walked aimlessly now for who knows how long and in the process, I've gotten myself further from the hotel than I wanted to be. I found a bench on a corner at a bus stop and decided to just rest a minute and get my bearings. Elbows on knees and head in hands, I just sat there a while and tried to think. For some reason, I was no longer thinking about how to find Di. I was thinking about how to fly back to California without her. I was thinking about talking to Susan face to face, about nosey Kaye and the apartment and moving her stuff out. I was thinking about going on without her in my life. The thought of not ever knowing where she is started to become a reality to me and it gave me such an empty feeling I wished I could die.

Now, I pictured her face and thought about her with such intense sorrow, and I knew she has never seen me this way and would never want to see me this way. Somehow, I told myself, I must give myself a push to get off this bench and make my way to the station. I hoped for the best and at the same time, I must be prepared for the worst. A huge city bus came to a halt in front of me and opened its doors. I looked up and waved the driver on and could see the irritation on his face for making an unnecessary stop. I forced myself up and walked in the direction of the tallest

188

building I saw.

It was probably close to noon as I walked up the steps to the police station. Streams of people were coming down as I was going up the stairs. There were lunch trucks and food vendors gathering out front and everyone was laughing and talking as I went against the tide into the building. I was thinking about the office where I work and how nothing gets done through the lunch hour and wonder why I'm doing this. Maybe I should turn around and go back over to the hotel and get my phone and have something to eat. As much as I wanted my phone, I dread the responsibility it is going to give me to respond to all the inquiries of all the well-meaning people that want to know the same thing I want to know - has anyone found Diane? So, I just decided to find myself a bench in the building somewhere and camp out.

I headed up to the second floor and sat on the same bench that I sat on yesterday. Maybe if I sit here long enough, my old friend James will find me and I will not have to hunt him down. Probably fifteen minutes passed and out he came.

"Brad my man, where have you been, I called your cell, but you didn't answer?"

His comment hit me right in the stomach so hard you could have punched me and it wouldn't have hurt any worse. He had this poker face look about him and I couldn't tell if this was good or bad. My nerves were in overdrive; I was somewhere between anger and passing out. I had prepared myself all morning for some kind of news and now that I heard he has tried to call me, I'm not sure I want to hear why. I must have turned white or something because he stepped forward to brace me at the elbow and usher me down the hall.

"Brad, you really have to relax. Remember I told you we are all working hard on this case?"

I just mumbled some agreeable answer as he headed for one of the offices at the end of the hall.

James pushed the door open and I focused for one quick moment on a woman behind the desk and then one long moment on the back of another woman's head. I saw some matted dirty- looking blond hair and the whole thing doesn't register until she turned her head to see who just entered the room. James put his hand on my shoulder and gave it a manly sort of squeeze as he backed away and I dropped down to chair height to give D the biggest hug she's ever had. I let go just enough to check out her face and touch her cheek to make sure this was all real. D's arm was around my back and clutching Bob and as she released the grip on him, he hit the linoleum floor, bounced and skidded the distance of the room. The noise jolted us as we watched him skid to a halt when he hit the wall.

"Poor guy, he's been through a lot."

"No Brad, we have all been through a lot. He can be replaced, but one thing I've learned over the last twenty four hours, there is no way I can ever replace you."

Made in the USA
Middletown, DE
01 February 2020